IN THE
WINDOW
ROOM

BOOK I OF THE HISTORIES OF EARTH

Katie,
Enjoy the adventure!

IN THE WINDOW ROOM

A NOVEL BY STEVEN J. CARROLL

ILLUSTRATIONS BY CHAD LEWIS
EDITED BY CLAIRE FORRESTER

-GLOBE LIGHT PRESS-
FOREST FALLS, CA

In the Window Room
Globe Light Press :

Globe Light Press

Globe Light Press
Printed in the United States of America

For questions regarding large or bulk orders of this book please address: Globe Light Press, Globelightpress@gmail.com

Connect with other window room fans:
facebook.com/inthewindowroom
www.stevenjcarroll.com

Interior design by Creios Design Co.

For those who seek out true adventure,
and wish to find it.

Acknowledgements

Thanks to all those who helped in the editing process, and to Chad Lewis for his very appreciated artwork. Also, thanks to Claire Forrester who helped edit this new edition.

And a very special thanks to Bre, my dear, gorgeous wife, for her inspiration and gracious encouragement, and also to author Toby Hoff, who through his dedication encouraged me to write a book of my own.

PROLOGUE

There was once a war, the first of its kind, unprecedented in its scope and size. And it was during this war that a middle-aged corporal was killed while leading a charge against the enemies' defenses.

All that day, and into the night, artillery had fallen on the nearby city of Arras, France. And for this reason, he stood before his men, while they hid in a secluded forest grove: speaking about courage, and about orders that had not come, and would not come in time, and about difficult decisions of conscience. He said that their allies' tunnels had been surrounded and compromised, and that he would be leading an assault that night in hopes to break the enemy line, and in order to save the lives of many men. And when he had concluded his speech he'd asked for volunteers, and there were only a few soldiers who'd stayed behind.

Yet, their attack that night, across the open field and under heavy fire, while successful, was not without loss. And because of this, the following day an officially sealed letter was sent home to England, to a new widow, and her young daughter; A letter that they had hoped to never receive, one that had brought many tears, and much sadness.

And as will sometimes happen, when faced with such circumstance as this, the young girl spent far too much time locked away in her room, staring out her window, hoping that a newer letter might arrive, to say that there had been a mistake and that everything would be alright. And the widow would spend all her time grieving, and was becoming of no good use as a mother, and would not allow herself to be happy again, although this was not her conscious choice.

So that therefore, the girl's aunt recommended a well-renowned school in Mayfield, where they were regarded for their discipline, insisting that the girl's mother should "think of what was best for the child."

However, this school could not be what that girl had needed. She was not in need of discipline, nor of a snobby boarding school where she would be away from her mother, and where she would find it difficult to make friends. What she had needed most of all was not a *what* at all, but a whom, and something that no school on earth could give to her.

IN THE WINDOW ROOM

CHAPTER ONE

THE GOVERNESS

N othing could be said for Delany Calbefur. She was guilty. Guilty as sin and she knew it, and dreadfully that knowledge did not make her laborious steps to the governor's office at all enjoyable. That is to say, a presumably guilty person has, at least, their half-believed excuses to help break the tension; being that, after all, blame in its own way can be nearly enjoyable. But a certainly guilty person, as was Miss Delany Calbefur, would most certainly be punished, and no amount of excuse making could deny that.

Her grainy steps made echoes against the walls of the courtyard. And the day, not as cold as it should have been this late in the season, as grown-ups would often say, felt colder on her face because of the light wind, and because of a few pools of tears that began forming in her eyes as she skidded her feet across the cobble stone.

(Here, if I may, I'd like to offer an aside note to the reader: As much as possible, within the pages of this book, I shall try to refrain from adding details or observations that only grown-ups would find interesting. This will not be that sort of book. And further, the adventures to be found within should not be cheapened by speaking of them in the ways that most older people speak of adventures.)

So, as it was, she walked begrudgingly through the courtyard and up a narrow stairway, till she came face to face with fate: the large old wood door of the governor's office. In truth, Lady Hanessy was a governess, although no living soul at the Mayfield house would dare call her that. In fact, some of the other girls at the house could be perfectly horrid with the names they'd fashioned for Hanessy. The worst offender being a rude girl by the name of Suzy Leeching, who had called her some unrepeatable name just last Thursday. And so, as Delany stood in awe of what she was about to do, firming her shaking hand into a sore fist and lifting it up to the weight of that immense door, and wondering why not one of the girls who had deserved this more than her shouldn't be here instead, she heard just the voice she had least wished to hear.

"You're late," came a shrill voice through the door, the sharpness of which nearly sent all the queasiness in her stomach shooting through her nose. With a determined sigh she twisted the icy handle, then stepped inside the cramped office.

"Yes, Governor Hanessy, but I was told to pack my things, and-" she stammered.

"No. None of that. I've no time for excuses, and even less for the girls who make them," interrupted Lady Hanessy. "What was this I heard today, about you and that Hardy girl? Your professor says you made quite a scene during recreation."

"Yes, but..." said Delany, about to muster up a protest, until her eyes caught the stern-faced glare of the Governess.

"Yes, Governor. I hit her," she said, lowering her head.

"So you did, and you will learn that violence will not be tolerated here at Mayfield," announced Hanessy, rather forcefully. "Would you like to offer Hardy your apology?"

Against bitten lip she managed to say, "Yes, Governor…" But with no response, so she added, "Will that lessen my punishment?"

"No. It won't," said Hanessy abruptly. "Your punishment should remain the same, no matter if you two came strolling in, hand in hand."

"Then am I to be sent home?"

"Certainly not!" issued the Governess. "I will not have it out that Mayfield cannot control their pupils. You will learn to behave, and I will see to it. And furthermore, since you cannot be trusted to keep well enough alone... alone is where you will be kept," Hanessy said, shuffling the papers on her desk.

And after what seemed a long silence, in which Delany kicked the back of her heels together to subside the rising queasiness she was beginning to feel again, the Governess continued, pursing her wrinkled lips together and looking up from her well papered desk, "You, Miss Calbefur, will spend the rest of the quarter alone, in the old Greyford house, after which you may return to your dormitory, if I think it beneficial."

At those words, Delany felt her stomach sink almost to the floor. She knew that the rest of the quarter meant a full month to the day from today, and who could survive a month in the old Greyford house, alone?

CHAPTER TWO

THE GREYFORD HOUSE

T he next morning, she was led down the dirt pathway, away from the main house, to the front of the old white slatted Victorian home. That is to say, what was once a white house, but was now so chipped and cracked it looked more dusty gray than white.

The fallen leaves in the yard blew up onto her shoes, as she stood gazing through the hazy windows. A look of shock was in Delany's eyes, and all the strange stories she'd heard whispered about this old place came creeping back into her mind.

"Come on, dear. It's not as bad as all that," said Maid Allen, the woman who had led Delany to the Greyford house that morning. Delany couldn't speak enough to give protest, and so the maid continued, "I remember when she was rather nice. Used to be a holiday home for travelers, till Mr. Greyford died and it'd fallen into disrepair."

"Was he... in the house when he died?" Delany asked, horrified.

"Deary, no, no," she chuckled. "He died in a hospital, and won't be coming back here, I assure you."

The simple fact that most all places can be associated with some dead person or another did not seem to console her, but to Delany's credit the front door creaked in just the right way as to make any place seem eerie.

The house was large and empty, the sort of place with covered furniture, and rooms leading to other unexpected rooms. (Which may be exciting given the right company, but for Delany, alone in this strange house, it was looming and unsettling.)

Clap. Clap.

Up the stairs, Maid Allen led her. The maid's hard-soled shoes thudding atop each step. She led her through an angled hallway, and up one more large step to the brightest room she had seen yet, with wide windows.

"This'll be your room," the old woman said. "I set out a fresh set of sheets for you when I heard the news last ev'n." And leaning in she said, "I also heard what that bitter girl said about your father, too. And although I'd be wrong for it, you can be sure I'd have swung at her as well." And there was a twinkle in the old woman's eye, that Delany took for solidarity. Then she continued, "After all, it's not as if he'd started that war, himself... and I don't think he should be blamed for fighting in it, either."

"Thank you," Delany said, breathing a sigh of relief, and feeling the first bit of comfort she'd felt in weeks. She set her bag down on the linen bed sheets and began to fumble with the clasp.

And calling behind her as she left, the maid exclaimed, "If you hear any noises at night, it's just these old pipes."

CHAPTER THREE
STRANGE DISCOVERIES

The next few days were surprisingly refreshing. To the rest of the girls at the main house, Delany appeared to be a conquering heroine with brave stories of illusive noises and intriguing discoveries. Even Mattie Hardy had come around to offer her own apologies for what she'd said to Delany just a few days prior, and less regretfully than one may have expected, Delany accepted them.

The old house was slowly becoming less foreboding with each opened curtain, and with each uncovered piece of furniture. But it took hours to finish exploring even a single room. Every new desk was filled with some pile of strange stones, odd figurines, or rolled up maps, charting out some unfamiliar chain of islands.

One afternoon, while she was busy searching, she came upon a massive painting, more alike in size to a tapestry than to a normal painting. It covered the length of one entire wall, and though it seems peculiar to say, she was fortunate to have found it. Down one set of stairs, and up another, in a wide sloping attic-style room, she happened to fling open the curtain of what appeared to be a small attic window, which to her wonderment was a passage way to yet another large room.

This "window room", as she called it, was not much unlike any other room in that great house, except for three obvious differences: For one, it was circular with high ceilings and no windows, save for a few small ones very near the roof. Secondly, none of the furniture was covered in blankets. And thirdly, and most impressively, was the painting. Covering half the room and stretching from floor to ceiling, it was the grandest painting Delany had ever seen, like the combination of the most lifelike atlas mixed with charts of stars that she was sure glowed somewhat on their own. Along the sides of the map were painted scenes of famous battles, and glorious cities. This room was the most difficult to leave.

All the same, it was not till much later that evening, lying in her bed, thinking of those glowing stars (for she was sure by now they were indeed glowing), that Delany realized the significance of the uncovered furniture.

"*What if I'm the only one still alive who knows that room exists?*" she thought.

She was too excited for sleep, and thus resolved herself to stay up all through the night. Howbeit, as anyone who has tried can tell you, the worst thing one can do to stay awake is to try at it, and just before she was fast asleep she half-pondered that those old pipes were rather noisier tonight than usual.

CHAPTER FOUR

AFTER MIDNIGHT

N ot long after midnight, she was awakened suddenly from her sleep by a series of crashing noises coming from the floor below hers. But for reason of her now helplessly tired eyes, Delany had nearly resolved herself that that loud racket was merely the latter part of a bad dream, or her own somewhat preoccupied imagination, and began again to fall heavily into sleep. Till she was jolted awake by a singular clank, coming from where she was now sure must be the downstairs kitchen.

Those noises made her fright, sitting up in her bed, being sure to lift her bedsheets up to her nose. She knew for certain they could not be the creaking pipes, and wondered again whether or not this house may actually have been haunted after all: and how inconvenient it would be to have an angry ghost chasing her around such a maze of a house.

The back of her neck was chilled. Sitting up in bed made it more difficult to wrap up warmly, and besides this she was scared. Furthermore, the old Greyford house was, by now, at least tolerable during daylight hours. But here, in the dim light of the moon, Delany was forced to travel around by candlelight; The hallways were too windy to walk about well at night without it, as she had not yet memorized the electrical switches.

So with all the strength she could measure, she began to inch her toes to the floor, and then to her slippers. Fortunately, there was a set of matches in the bedside drawer along with a fresh candlestick. Then, breathing in deeply, the match was struck, and she proceeded to the bedroom door, cautiously turning the knob, and being sure to not let the bolt click on her way out.

Darkness seemed to crowd around every corner as she crept through the upstairs hall, and at every open doorway she made eager promises to shut each one of them tightly the next morning. Her heart beat in a flutter. She gasped quietly in the stillness, and when she came to the stairway the shadows jutted out in an obstinate manner, playing tricks with her eyes.

At the first step, she almost lost her footing, but managed to catch herself abruptly by the railing. A bit angrily, she stiffened up straight to listen. "*Had he heard?*" she thought to herself, not realizing what a task it would be to actually come upon a ghost by surprise.

After this, her steps were much more deliberate, and soon she found herself safely down, staring at a clearly defined column of light shining through the kitchen door; and in the emptiness of that old, ramshackled house she could hear strange noises drifting in through the open doorway. (I call them strange here, because although the sounds themselves were quite normal and easily distinguishable: the tinkering of plates while preparing a meal, and the earthy hum of a pleasant folk tune. To anyone who'd fully expected ghoulish, ghastly haunts, even these familiar tones can seem strange.)

Now you must not think Delany rash here for what is to happen next; Being, for the most part, not easily frightened on account of her stubbornness. Delany was, however, altogether sick of being afraid that night. Presently convincing herself that the sounds of a late supper being prepared that night must have been caused by Maid Allen, who surely would have come to check on her, and was now helping herself to whatever wares were left over in the kitchen.

All at once, she picked up her steps and came bustling into the kitchen, laughing as only one does when they are truly unnerved but wish to hide it.

"Maid Allen, why are you…" she stopped. There was no one in the room, and the door of the ice box was left wide open. "…not here?" she concluded.

Just then, with a short heaving sound, the door to the ice box was flung shut. And before her stood a large rodent-like animal, just tall enough to reach the lower compartment handle on the box if he were to stand on the tips of his toes. He was holding a plate of sandwich meats.

"Did I wake you?" the thing said politely.

CHAPTER FIVE

SECRET PASSAGES

H er candle was thrown from her hand as Delany went screaming from the kitchen, tripping up the darkened stairway. Till she came fumbling to her room, securely bolting the door behind her. She stood hunched, panting feverishly. She was safe.

But this was not to last for long. A subtle wheeling sound could be heard from inside the closet at the far side of the room; and she would not have that thing to run around her ankles in the dark. So she quickly switched on the bedside lamp, and stood atop her bed, making sure to first grab the largest and heaviest pillow she could find.

Eek. The wheeling noise had stopped, and she could see that creature's paw slowly push open the closet door. With a yelp she hurled her pillow, slamming it shut again.

"Go away!" she cried.

"It's just... I've realized what an awful introduction I've made for myself," said a voice from inside the closet. There was no response. So timidly the creature eased at the door again, and began walking open armed into the room.

"Allow me to introduce mysel---f." Another pillow hit him squarely in the face.

"Get out!" Delany exclaimed.

11

"I come in peace," he said, his muffled voice from beneath the pillow.

"Do you promise?" she asked.

"Yes," he said, peering out from the corner of the pillow, "…and do you promise not to throw things at me?"

"I guess so…" she said.

The little thing let out a deep breath. "Well, I suppose that will have to do," he said, throwing off the pillow and scurrying up the bedside. They both sat down cross-legged at opposite ends of the bed and he began again, but stopped, thinking of perhaps something better to say.

Leaning his face into his tiny paw, he said, "I believe these things go along much better over supper. Would you like me make you a plate?" he said, motioning to the closet. "It's no trouble."

Delany graciously declined. But before she could finish thanking him for his offer the little thing had noisily waddled into the closet, and was back before she knew it, carrying with both hands a hefty plate of turkey and sliced cheeses.

"Just in case you change your mind," he said. "I'd nearly forgot my appetite, what with all the screaming downstairs." His stubby tail wiggled as he slid a very sizable late dinner up onto the bed.

"You know, there's nothing that can ruin a conversation better than an empty stomach," he said, through a bite of provolone. "You know it's like I always-"

"How did you do that?" Delany interrupted. "Is it some sort of trick door or… magic?"

"Oh that. No, it's not magic," he said, his mouth full, and with a piece of turkey in his hand. "There are secret passages all around you if you know where to look for them."

Delany's eyes lit up. "Like the one in the attic?" she asked. The little mammal stopped chewing. "...the one that looks like a window?" she continued.

A wide-faced grin crept onto her furry companion's face, not the sort of grin one gives out of contempt, but the kind most related to pride.

"So we've found something interesting to talk about then," he said.

Until this point, she had not thought it possible for animals to smile (which still may be the case). However, this was no ordinary animal. This one looked as though he knew a story worth listening to.

CHAPTER SIX

A LATE-NIGHT STORY

T he following is a revision of the rest of that night's conversations, in order that the reader might better understand the main points of his story. Left out are quite a number of unimportant side stories from which the teller was constantly needing to be brought back from. He began his story much like this:

"Many years ago, when I was much more of a pup than I am now, Arthur Greyford ran what some would call a holiday home for distant travelers, *very* distant... from other worlds."

He spoke the latter part of this more slowly, to emphasis its importance. Delany, however, did not catch this and thought she could correct him. "You mean 'from around the world', right?"

"No," he said, with a chuckle. "I mean what I said." Taking a bite more of cheddar, he continued, "Arthur was a business man, if ever I'd seen one..." [Here he went on at length about how it's become considerably easier to sell things these days, on account that most folks don't really know what's needed.] After which he said, "So when he'd made as much money as any reasonable chap would want, and because he'd no kin to look after, he retired, in a manner of speaking. Setting himself to the occupation of travel and of collecting, the very rare and the very valuable."

[At this point, Delany interrupted the furry orator's story to ask why Mr. Greyford hadn't any surviving relatives. In most situations, this would have been met with a quick response. But considering he'd had relatively few house guest recently, and was rather enjoying himself, he began to talk about how sometimes the things you might wish for, and the things that actually happen, can be quite different. What Delany gathered though, in between chewed morsels, was that the late Mrs. Greyford had suffered a fever during childbirth some years prior, and that Mr. Greyford had decided to remain unmarried.]

"Where were we?" he asked, scratching the hair on his cheek. "Oh, yes," he said. "The funny thing about collecting though is, that if you aren't careful with it, you may find things that are actually worth something, and that was his [Arthur's] case."

Delany was so excited at this point, that she knew what he might mention next, that she blurted out in amazement, "So that's how he found the painting?"

"Yeah, I suppose you could say it like that," wiping the crumbs from his whiskers. "Or more likely, rather, it was the painting that found him. You see it's not your average piece of artwork, it is... more like a motion picture than the ordinary, everyday still kind."

Just then a very eager rooster began to crow, and Delany realized her room was not so dark as it had once been. "It's late," she said with a yawn, as she leant back against the headboard.

"Or early," said the marmot, who had nearly finished his plate by then and was looking just a bit plumper than before.

"You know, child, I haven't properly introduced myself yet," he said.

Delany, who had listlessly slid down into a large fluffy pillow, could not let this go, even as tired as she was. So she responded, "I'm not a child," her face scrunched to the side, looking very much like a child.

"Alright then, what should I call you?" he replied.

In an effort to redeem herself, she sat up, trying to appear much more awake than she really was. "Oh, I don't know..." she said. "My name is Delany, but my friends like to call me Del."

"And I'm Meris," he said. Then lifting up the plate in front of him, "Would you like the last piece?" he asked.

The pair had been awake for hours by then. So relatively speaking it was well past breakfast time, and under normal circumstances, Delany might have refused a slice of gouda offered to her by a rodent. But since she had never met a talking animal before, and being so dreadfully hungry, she obliged.

"I guess so," she said.

CHAPTER SEVEN

THE NEXT DAY

A ll the next day, two things withheld Delany from believing her midnight meeting with that fuzzy creature hadn't all been some strange dream: For one, being that they had ended their talk so late (or early depending on your point of view), Delany had not been allowed to fall back asleep. And secondly, because of that, she was miserably tired the whole day, a good enough sign to her and to anyone else that she'd had precious little sleep the night before.

One of those who had noticed her obvious lack of sleep that day was Mattie Hardy. She had sat behind her during a lecture on photosynthesis that morning in science course, and was a good enough sport to kick her chair as the professor came near their row. Delany was surprised, and grateful. Mattie had not taken her chance to spite her, even though she very well could have. Which made Delany wonder that perhaps she had not hit her as hard as she thought.

"You saved my life," Del said, while fighting back the urge to give a noticeable stretch.

"Just try to keep your eyes open, then..." Mattie whispered, with a failed attempt at harshness, the kind you may try at when you've done something nice and would, just as well, not like to be congratulated for it.

Delany sat upright. Still mostly bored, and altogether too tired to concentrate on the lesson, she started to think about how Mattie was not as mean to her as she thought she should have been. Soon another queasy feeling began stirring inside Delany's stomach. Although, not completely unlike her feelings of guilt just a few days prior, this newly unsettled feeling could be compared more precisely to the feeling you may have if you'd invited a new friend home for dinner, and then realized your kitchen table was a squalor, and not at all as clean as you'd remembered. Delany was confused and could not help but think, no matter how hard she tried, that she had done something wrong.

(Whatever that thing was that Delany felt, and however it had happened, I believe it is important to note here that it was at this exact moment the two girls first let off being enemies. Don't misunderstand however, the two were still very much at odds with each other, and would be for quite some time, but they were no longer enemies, not in any unchangeable sense. And, although some may argue differently, I believe it was here, also, that the pair first began to become friends.)

The rest of the day at Mayfield was an uneventful blur, and to tell the truth Delany was glad to see it go. The usually long walk back from main house to Greyford was moving along, this evening, at a hurried pace. But she was still a good distance away, staring up at the faded white house, when a sudden flash of light broke through a tiny slatted gable window. At the sight of this, Delany ran up the lawn, and burst open the front door, too excited for walking.

"Meris," she said breathlessly. "Meris, are you here?"

The house was noiseless. She shut the door, and began to search through each tangled room. "Come out, Meris!" she yelled, but there was no reply. Each winding hall and each forgotten study, was as lifeless as the one before.

A little bewildered, she decided to make her way up to the attic. "Here, squirrel…" she said, as she peered through the curtain, looking hopefully into the window room.

The massive colored painting shone starlight onto her face, but there was no one there. So finally, when she had convinced herself there was no one to be found, disheartened and alone, Delany slunk back downstairs, helping herself to half a piece of leftover dutch apple pie. And, thoroughly exhausted, laid her head down on the dining table, and fell asleep.

(Now the reader should note that, at this point, Delany was not a very keen naturalist. So that when she called Meris a squirrel, what she actually meant by it was "ground squirrel". Although, it could be supposed, that if she'd been raised in a place that had them, she might have referred to her houseguest as a gopher, but even that would not have been the closest approximation. For as anyone can tell you, who's been a student of North American zoology, what Meris was most akin to, in our world, would be the Gunnison's prairie dog, only proportionally much larger. Granted, however, if it helps to think of him as a somewhat larger and stockier ground squirrel, then I suppose no real harm has been done.)

That evening, Delany awoke to an odd, slippery sort of sound, and saw that it was that clever marmot, dragging a newly cut block of ice across the kitchen floor. His little furry face grunting and sweating, and his hooded parka zipped up to the top.

"Would you like a hand with that?" she asked.

He was now pushing at it with all his might, and slipping a bit as the ice melted. "If you don't mind," he strained. "Ice seems to have gotten heavier now-a-days…"

As it turned out, the weighty block was even a struggle for Del to lift up into the ice box on her own. So that, in the end, the two managed to hoist it up into the compartment, but only after the count of three, and with very chilled, wet hands.

When they had finished, Meris wiped the beads of sweat from his forehead and collapsed, his back against the metal ice box.

Delany's school uniform was now entirely soaked through with water, and was remarkably unpleasant, but it was for this reason that she realized something peculiar, something she probably should have noticed minutes ago.

It hadn't yet snowed at Mayfield. It hadn't even been cold enough for it. *"How in the world could he have brought such a large piece of ice into the house all by himself?"* she wondered.

"Where did you get that?" she asked, pointing her finger to the compartment above his head.

Meris seemed befuddled by her question.

"The icebox?…" he replied.

"No, of course not," she said, looking somewhat perturbed. "I mean the ice. Where did you get it from?"

Meris, who until then was playing as if he'd been feverishly exhausted, suddenly perked his ears. A clear glint shone in his eyes.

"Would you like to see?" he asked.

But before he'd given her a chance to answer this he was up, and calling out from the hall for her to follow him and to keep up, and that she was the one that was so curious about it, and that he didn't know why she was being so slow.

Delany ran as fast as she could to keep up, slipping across the wood in her laced shoes. Her new friend was a pudgy creature, but fast as a jack-rabbit if the opportunity presented itself. Bounding up the stairs, and through the mazing halls, Delany just managed to catch a glimpse of him at every turn. Fortunately, for her, she had a good notion of where they were headed; and, as it turned out, she was right.

When she landed at the attic's threshold, she could just make out the slightest flap in the tiniest window curtain in the room. Many would have thought it to be the most insignificant draft, or would have missed it altogether. But Delany had it in mind where they were headed, and so she knew what to look for.

CHAPTER EIGHT
INTO THE WINDOW ROOM

I t is one thing to have mysterious adventures thrust upon you, by happenstance, and it is quite another to go looking for them. Delany knew that if she entered into the window room she would certainly be confronting adventure in the face, and there was no turning back from that. She breathed, a deep readying breath, and scrambled into the passage.

It was well into evening by then, and the thin, slated windows near the roof let in almost no light at all, still the room was not blackened. An immensity of light burst from the painting. The stars obviously glowed, like they had before, but because of the darkness around her, Del could notice that light, like daylight, was pouring from many of the scenes painted near the edges. Vignettes of regal walled cities and titanish battles gleamed rays of light into the room. Scenes that had been painted in night, when she last saw them, were now images of morning sunrises, and what had been a depiction of a well-lit mountain glade was now sprinkled with night. Her mouth opened wide, but said nothing.

Meris hardly noticed her standing there, as he fiddled and poked around an antique looking globe, which was oddly positioned in precisely the exact center of the room.

He was searching for something that must have been undeniably lost, by the way he squiggled and squirmed looking through every hidden drawer.

"Ah ha! There it is," he said with excitement. Then, turning to Del, "The Mrs. would always say to me, 'You'd lose your tail if you wasn't sitting on it…'" Meris laughed a slight laugh at this, although Del was still unsure whether or not he hadn't made himself sadder for laughing. Albeit, she did not have time to think about that, considering what happened next was almost too magnificent to be believed.

The globe was an odd, rugged and sturdy piece of furniture, much too wide to reach round the entirety of it on your own, but not so big that Meris wouldn't be able to touch the top if he stood tip-toed on the thick equatorial rim that spanned its center. Along the rim were a variety of knobs and dials. They appeared to be functional, like the switches and dials on a radio, but were much more ornately complicated than anything Del had seen before.

Somewhat out of place however, near the right side of the globe, was a rather ordinary looking brass crank. This was that same item Meris had so excitedly found just a few moments before, and had fit precisely into the side of the globe with a clever smile. Still, the crank was so plain that Del hadn't even noticed it, until she had first looked over every other more interesting feature she could find.

In the meantime, Meris had busied himself around a very cluttered desk to the right of the painting. He was mumbling to himself as he peered over a large leather-bound book filled with charts, and degree markings, and coordinates. Every now and then he would stop abruptly to check a desk clock, or to slide weights and measurements across an elaborate abacus.

"There, that'll do well enough," he said, stepping down from his chair.

He then waddled over to the globe, and began turning knobs and flipping switches. Delany was still horribly confused, so she said nothing for a while. Till, at last, it occurred to her to ask a very reasonable sounding question.

"Shouldn't I go fetch my coat…" she asked, then added, "…if we'll be somewhere out in the snow?"

"Ha!" the furry creature exclaimed. "I've got more sense than that to send us traipsing across frozen wasteland on your first time out. Surely wouldn't be worth much as a guide if I did that."

She watched as the last switch was flipped. All at once the luminous painting was completely transformed, like the turning of a page. Every star chart, and every geographical map was swept away to reveal a completely new world. Even the lighted pictures near the edges were replaced with new civilizations and new wonders.

"Then, where are we going?" she asked nervously, glancing at her squirrel friend. "Some place completely safe I hope…"

He didn't respond immediately. Instead he stooped down, reached his paw into a tiny hidden drawer near the globe's base, and pulled out an ornate dagger. It was child sized, but not a toy, with an intricately decorated woven sheath and band, which he flung around his shoulder, letting the dagger hang confidently at his side.

"No one is ever completely safe, Del," he said, with a reassuring tone in his voice. "Yet, where we're headed is safer than most."

Then, grasping onto the brass crank, he began to turn the handle as fast as he could. There was no turning back.

CHAPTER NINE

A NEW JOURNEY

The turning made a repetitive whirling noise, like the propellor of a plane when it's been started. Del knew there must have been some fanciful mechanism at work within the globe, because she could hear gears ticking and high-pitched buzzes coming from inside. The room grew brighter. The globe was now glowing in a similar way to the painting, like a light bulb slowly brightening.

Another thing she noticed, at this moment, was that bands of soft colored light began to spin out from the machine in circular waves. As they continued, the colors became more apparent, and they were accompanied by sounds, tones that might be compared to the sound of concert bells being played by a sunrise. It was the most glorious music Del had yet heard in her lifetime.

Meris let go of the crank, jumped up onto the wooden control board that spanned the center of the globe, and pointed to an exact place on the map.

"Put your hands right… there," he said in his loudest voice, trying to be heard above the sounds of the light, and the whirling and ticking coming from inside the globe.

"Right here?" Del asked, as she spread her hands out, trying to clarify the exact spot.

"That's it!" he yelled. "Wouldn't want to end up in an ocean, now would we?"

This last comment may have ended their travels altogether. That is, if Del hadn't already begun to place her hands upon the globe (and truth be told, it's uncertain whether or not she was even able to hear him by this point). The sounds of the machine made a water-falling roar inside the window room, and it only grew louder the instant her hands touched the globe.

A single column of golden sunlight shot upwards toward the ceiling: beams breaking through the cracks of her fingers.

The loud buzzing noises began to heighten in pitch. "Hold on!" he yelled, and put out his hand for comfort. Del grabbed ahold of his little furry paw.

She began to float. They were both being pulled into the air, suspended within a glowing orb of light. They were a few meters above the floorboards by now. Del was as scared as she'd ever been, but not the sort that makes you cry. The queasiness came back into her stomach, and she wondered what she had gotten herself into.

The ticking, and the sound of the light beams lessened. The painting ahead of them was alive with vibrant color. The room was awash in radiant light.

All at once, the pair burst toward the painting, as if being exploded from a cannon. And almost so quickly that you might not have seen it happen at all, the room was gone, and there was blackness and faint dots of light.

"Ahhh!" Delany screamed in the silence around them.

She had meant to panic as soon as she had seen herself being rushed toward the painting. Howbeit, because of the sheer speed at which the two were now traveling it had taken her these several moments to get her body to do

26

what she had wanted it to.

What made matters worse for her, was that her furry companion did not at all seem bothered by the circumstances; and, in fact, looked wryly amused by her reaction. So that all the more unsteadily, Del began to scream, well more than she had initially intended. Until at last, when she had had her fill of panicking, she paused in silence, and became more alert, and in awe of the seemingly infinite magnitude around her.

Meris chuckled to himself. "Well you sure are making an awful fuss about it, aren't you?" She was speechless, taking in the black expanse of space. "No need to worry, love. The worst of it is over," he said.

Now she could finally see what was going on. Her eyes had adjusted to the light. And she was more at ease, after hearing that the worst was behind her. She was being rocketed through space, watching stars and clouds of stars, planets and close suns pass her by, much like you may do if you've gone out for a ride in a train through the countryside. Only Del knew enough of science by then to understand this: that she must have been traveling at an enormous speed, faster than you could ever imagine. A colossal red planet and clusters of ringed colored moons flew by her in an instant. The beauty of the universe was overwhelming.

The orb of golden light by which they were traveling made positively no sound at all. There was neither wind nor the sound of motion, nothing echoed, even her breath seemed louder. Very rarely is one faced with that level of silence, the kind which has the tendency to make even our quietest thoughts more apparent. In a similar way, as well, this unnoised place began to take its effect. Gazing intently now at a distant nebulas, Del wondered more openly, much about secret thoughts she had tried very dearly to keep hidden these past few months (partially for reason of her deep set need to feel strong enough to handle things on her own, and also because of what her mother had told her, that "...we mustn't pity ourselves, believing in fairy tales"). Still, quite a number of unbelievable things had recently been presented to Del, and when combined with the immeasurable presence of complex beauty she was now seeing, it gave her, all the more, courage to hope in those "fairy tales", as her mother called them.

"Can we get to heaven from here?" she asked, turning to Meris.

However, he did not answer her question right away, and seemed to be thinking very diligently about it for some moments, rubbing his cheek with his palm.

"Yes, we can, Del," he said. "But not in the same way I think you mean it."

CHAPTER TEN
A MORNING IN THE GLADE

The two came to rest, safely in a wide green glade, on a planet not much unlike our own. Though, scientifically speaking, it was approximately seven-eighths the size of ours, but that was, reasonably, the least of her concerns as their orb bolted through the cloud cover. Delany was nervous, and her face would have certainly given her away, if not for the fact that she was trying very hard to disguise it; and the reason for this being that, as she could tell, that little gopher was being so annoyingly confident about the whole process.

Still, the orb, which had been slowing for some time now, reduced its pace to a gentle glide, and the two landed on their feet in a pleasant late spring meadow. It was morning, the air was still wet with dew. Overhead and around the glade could be heard the high chattering of nearby birds. Delany thought it good to hear those sounds, after being trapped in silence for what seemed like ages.

The morning sunrise shone robust above the tree line, and they quickly set out, exploring the open field. As they went along, the two let their hands fall among a patch of wild flowers, and felt the tickle of the petals on their fingertips.

"Are all worlds like this?" she asked.

"No, though I've often wished they could be."

Much to their surprise (although in a place like this it should have been nearly expected), at the far end of the glade, they found a cool, calm stream. Having found such a place the two morning wanderers didn't think it necessary to walk any further; and, without a moment's hesitation, the chubby gopher plopped down into a thick spot of tall grasses, helping himself to a breakfast of tender sweet violets, while Del unlaced her shoes to dip in her toes at the water's bank.

"I wish we'd never have to go back. I'd much rather be-"

Her words stopped cold. How she had meant to finish her sentence was like this: "I'd much rather be here than at Mayfield." But at the moment she turned her head towards the little ground squirrel, she noticed him staring straight at her, and how troubled he looked. He put a finger over his snout.

"Shhh! I think I heard something…"

Carefully and quietly he motioned to her to keep her head down, and to crawl through the tall grass to join him. She managed this, but rather unpleasantly. Regretting the whole time for having taken off her shoes, and in such an unfamiliar place.

Motionless and breathless, she watched as he stood up on his hind legs, his ears twitching and eyes straining to scan above the overgrowth.

"Do you hear anything?" she asked in faint whisper.

Again, he signaled for her to stay quiet. There was a long pause, a firm silence broken only by the passing songbird. Del deeply wished to ask her question again, but thought it better, and rightly so, to remain still.

When, at last, the noises had distilled, Meris crept up alongside her.

"I should never have brought you here. Not for this long at least."

"Is it gone?"

"Yes, I believe they are… I heard voices, across the meadow. Seem to have quieted down, and gone back the way they came."

"Voices?"

"AHH!!"

Suddenly there was a flash of red cloth, and the glittering of metal. There was rolling around, and kicking. Meris bit and clawed at whatever he could find; Being too caught off guard to get out his knife, so that, in the end, it was useless. The two hooded figures in chain mail wrestled them to the ground without much of a fight. They were scouts from the royal army, the golden eagle crest embroidered on their robes, and both of them hardened soldiers.

"There's a feisty one here," said the first soldier, holding the gopher up against his chest, held tightly with both arms.

Meris had just a few moments ago realized how incapable he was of prying himself free. So he hung there, kicking out his feet every so often, just to prove he was still trying.

"Let him go!" Delany squirmed, and gave another kick at the soldier who had her shoulders pinned.

"Ha! Not a chance, lil' misses. A good ole' trained rat like that'll fetch a nice price, when we get to court."

She wiggled as she spoke, "Yah, shows what you know. He's just a helpless little animal." This was a lie of course, but, at the time, it may have seemed more like a half-truth. After all, Meris did look rather worn out at the moment.

"Course he is, mum," said the soldier who was gripping the gopher firmly with both arms. "But I ain't never seen a helpless rat with a knife strapped to his back, that's for sure."

These two military men were rough, and coarse, not bearded, but by no means well shaven. And it occurred to Del that she may as well give in, thinking that these were not the sort of men you'd like to be running from.

CHAPTER ELEVEN

CAPTURED

T he morning gleam above the hills had burnt away the dew from off the long high grasses. It swept away the water collected atop the flower petals. Del had much enjoyed horseback riding, whenever she'd had the opportunity to go. In fact, she was actually quite a natural at it, considering how many few times her mother would allow her to take the train out towards Bedford, where her aunt lived. (In truth, Del's aunt and cousins were dreadful people, but she'd often tell herself that her aunt's two mares were darling, and that that made up for the fact.)

This morning's ride, however, was not at all enjoyable. For one, the air had warmed enough to be refreshing at an even trot, but at the speed they were galloping the wind grew chilled again. And secondly, because even though her captors had agreed to let her have her shoes, they were not, in the least, interested in her comfort or safety. And this could easily be seen by the way they drove the horses, and by how unconcernedly Del was forced up high onto the saddle.

Still, thankfully, within the hour, she could see a thin outline emerging from across the great plain, and as they drove on the outline became a city, and the walls grew higher and more defined; a regal sweeping city, with a well fortified wall made of massive tan colored stones. Beside this, spread out against the mountain range, lay a deep blue lake, glittering and calm. It was the kind of place one would never suspect evil of. Del wondered to herself, as they rushed toward the gate, how strange it was, then, that men like these would be allowed to live in such a beautiful place.

They flung through the gates, stopping only slightly for men and women in the streets, narrowly missing a few of them. At last they slowed and came halting at the palace gate.

"Ho, porter! Open up. King's business," yelled the man who'd held Meris.

An old man's voice answered back from behind the door, "Alright now, no need to go on shout'n, I'm not as deaf as all that." Creaking hinges and the sound of a chain let loose, the door gave a crack, and was opened.

The next few moments were extremely chaotic for the two hostages. Shoved and coerced past this guard and that, down and through dimly lit halls, the whole process was undeniably confusing. What Del did manage to derive, however, through several hushed conversations, was that they were to be considered spies, and as such the two hired soldiers that found them were to be given a reward, but not before they were made to pay off a few, very recent, debts.

In a similar manner, pushed and herded and sold, they were made to walk into a wide columned room, the king's throne ahead of them. Del's hands began to sweat. The king was slouched, yet sitting as high upon the throne as he could (how this is possible, I'm not quite sure). Greedily he set about working the meat off an early lunch, and he seemed to pay them no attention at all.

The grimy guard, who had led them both in, told them to stand a certain distance away. He then went ahead to whisper something into his majesty's fat ear.

"Eh… Spies!" the king exclaimed, briefly interrupting the guard's message.

Del strained to hear even the slightest syllable of the guard's story, but couldn't. Meris, who was always much better at this sort of thing, heard every word clearly, but pretended as if he hadn't.

"So, little girl," the king grinned. "You've come to kill me, have you?"

Del's eyes widened. "No, I swear. We haven't."

"Are you so sure?" he said wryly. "Then what is this?"

He held up a small object by its strap. Del recognized the weapon immediately, and her face gave her away. (This was, of course, the knife Meris had brought along with them that morning for safety's sake.)

"Ah. So it is true, then?"

"No! I promise... it's not!"

Until then, Del had never yet been before a king, but quickly realized, by the way he shifted in his seat as she spoke, that she would be unwise to raise her voice again. So she added, with greater restraint, " …Your Majesty."

At this point, the king's large face began to redden, and he looked as though he were going to yell, but stopped however, suddenly; beginning again, only this time in a rich, more gracious tone.

"My dear…" he said.

Del tried to fight back a rising tear. "Forgive me," he continued.

"I have been unconsciously rude this whole time. After all, you're not on trial here [he chuckled]. If you would just plainly tell me where you are from, and who sent you, then I'll let you go free… no harm done."

Del may have lied here, except that she hadn't even the faintest idea of where to start. And therefore, in the end, she decided the truth would be a safer bet.

"No one sent me... Your Majesty," she said.

"No one sent you?" he asked, as though falsely surprised. "So then, tell me, where are you from? And how did you end up in Miller's Glade, all by yourself, without a horse?"

"We flew there…" Although, she did not completely believe herself as she said it.

The king laughed, to himself. "Flew? Like a bird?"

"Yes, Your Majesty… well not quite," she began to explain.

"Little girl," his voice grew pointed, its pace quickened. "Do you think I am a fool? Do you now?"

"No, sir, I-"

Then suddenly, erupting from his chair like a fire, he yelled, "Then why do you treat me like one?!"

"Guards!" he shouted, motioning towards Del. "Take this spy away and clap her in irons, and bring that filth to the gardens [pointing at Meris]. At least, we may have some use for a trained rat."

CHAPTER TWELVE

ALONE

A lone, and feeling very much so, Del sat huddled against the far wall of her cell. She drew these thoughts around in her head: that no one at Mayfield would ever believe her if she were to tell them her story, and would she ever get home again to tell it?

The dirt floor of the prison was dirtier than most. Droplets of dripping water made the occasional beat. And all the many awful, monotonous lectures she'd yet withstood this quarter seemed like roses compared to this place. She was alone, her face scuffed with dirt.

Drop by drop, springs of despair, tides of indignation, began to roll over her thoughts. Even Suzy Leeching, with her grotesque pigtailed hair, Del would have welcomed with open arms, for she was very much alone (or at least seemed to be).

"What are you crying for? You just got here," said a voice from out in the hall.

(It was good fortune, indeed, that the jailor was a decent man; 'Didn't think it right to put a helpless girl in chains, who was obviously not going to hurt anyone.')

So at once, and cautiously, Del made her way over to the door, and peered through the open hatch. The dark prison hall was perfectly empty.

Still, in an attempt to justify herself, she said, "I wasn't crying." Although this was plainly untrue. Her voice was faint and scratched, for she had been crying.

"Sure you were," he repeated.

In an instant, Del saw whom the voice belonged to: a pair of eyes, young eyes, not much older than hers, were staring through the hatch directly across from her own.

"Do they think you're a spy too?" she asked.

"No," he said. Del could see his eyes look down, as he continued, "They think I'm a murderer."

There was a pause, in which Del tried very hard to think of a proper response, but not having much success, she asked, "Well… are you?"

"No," the prisoner replied. "Not any more than you are a spy."

Before this time, the thought that men and women could be locked away in prison, on false charges, never really occurred to her, and she was furious at the sort of justice that would allow for it.

"That wicked brute," she replied, referring to the king. "Who has he said you've killed then, that you haven't?"

"Our brother," he replied.

Del's mouth gave a gasp, though the other prisoner's eyes couldn't see this.

A summary of the prisoner, Corwan's, story, as she, at last, came to understand it: As he described, his name was Corwan, the third son of Reuel, a prince of the realm, and a true servant to his people. In a week's time he was to be taken before the high council, to stand trial for the murder of his eldest brother, who was also named Reuel. (Del did not, however, understand this at first, and had so thoroughly confused herself that Corwan was made to retell a good portion of his story from the beginning.)

After this, she came to realize that Faron, Corwan's middle brother (whom she was quite sure did not have the same name as anyone else in the story) was, almost certainly, the true murderer; And that all but one, of his eldest brother's most loyal generals had been executed on suspicion of treason, or had met some other dubious end.

Corwan's story, however, had to be cut short, towards the end, on account of Del's almost constant interruptions: "Is that just me?" she would say. "Can you hear that?" and "My word... that noise." To this, the prince would often repeat that he had no idea what noise she was referring to, that the prison was altogether deathly silent, and that she should, again, try to keep her voice down.

Light crept upon the cell walls like a sunrise, yet there were no windows. Bands of color swirled, breaking against the corners of the room. Then, suddenly, like a beam of light reflected from off a mirror, the roof of the prison broke away.

Stars and galaxies blurred around her. Her sides hurt. The air was pushed from her lungs by the sheer force of it, then blackness. She lay gasping, her hands pressed on wooden floorboards. She was back in the window room, alone.

CHAPTER THIRTEEN

BACK ON EARTH

The ground was frosted the next morning. She slipped in her leather laced boots, running up the hard sanded path. Del was late. How she could be in trouble in two worlds at the same time completely astonished her; and was positively exhausting, if you'd stop to think about it, but she could not, she was late.

As Del came rushing into the courtyard, her fears were confirmed. It was emptied. The bell had already been rung. The echos of her hurried steps clashed against the cobble stones, and they were these same echos that followed her up the stairwell and bounded through the hall, stopping abruptly at the door.

Perhaps, if she were mindful about it, she could sneak in unnoticed. It was worth the momentary encouragement to hope in such a thing, but these hopes were to be short lived.

"Miss Calbefur."

She froze. Every eye in the classroom turned to stare at her.

"Tardiness *will not* be tolerated in my classroom."

Del of course knew this, and therefore nodded apologetically, trying to make it to her seat without any further disturbance.

But this did not seem to appease her professor, who continued, "Since you have already squandered a good potion of the lecture… and have, as it seems, no appreciation for silence, please speak up and tell the class what's kept you."

"I was-" But before Del had the opportunity to explain herself she was interrupted again by her professor, who consequently had no real interest in hearing what she had to say.

"It was obviously of such *dire* importance as to keep you from your course work."

As a matter of fact, it had been. The fate of an entire kingdom, and now also the lives of her friends were hanging in the balance. But to explain such a thing or anything remotely like it to this buggish woman would have been a futile endeavor. So she said nothing, except what she knew from experience would set her in the least amount of trouble.

"Yes, Master Kaufield. It won't happen again."

Del had learnt, thus after a tough series of trials and error, that the thing adults had most liked to hear, more so than nearly every other thing in the world, was that "it [whatever *it* may be] will never happen again"; and she'd often used this to her advantage whenever she had the chance.

Later that day, during recreation period, Del sat by herself at the far end of the yard, her head buried in her hands. Her mind was overwhelmed. A lot now rested on her shoulders, and this had all happened so suddenly, and she hadn't asked for any of it.

She was in need of some magnificent plan to get back, and she was sure she needed more time. Even so, as it turned out, what Del had need of most, although she was simply unaware she had needed it, was a friend.

For this reason then it was good fortune indeed, that who should come to Delany's aid, but none other than Mattie Hardy. (Who was not as much of a friend as Del would have liked. Yet not necessarily a true enemy either, which made her, at least, a permissible candidate, as most would measure.)

"What's the matter?"

Mattie had left the other group of girls and was now, surprisingly, standing just a wide step's length in front of her. Del hadn't noticed her walk up, she had not been paying much attention. And it took her till the end of a deep breath to regain her composure.

"You startled me," she said.

"Oh. I'm sorry… [then glancing behind her] it's just we'd all wondered why you've been such a mess this week."

"So, they've sent you over here to check on me then?" Del replied.

Mattie furrowed her eyes at the notion. "No one sent me," she said. "It's just people were talking, coming up with their own ideas, and I didn't think that was right proper to do."

"Oh…" A perplexed sort of look came across Del's face, "But then if I tell you, you'll just go blabbing about me to all your friends."

"No I won't," she quickly replied. "Not if you didn't want me to…"

Here, under normal circumstances, Del would have begun to tell her story, except that she was not entirely convinced that this Hardy girl, who had just so recently been an outright enemy, would keep good on her word.

"Yah, and if I tell you something bonkers, the kind of thing people get teased their whole lives for, do you promise to keep it a secret then?"

"What is it?"

"Do you promise?" Del asked, an emphatic strain in her voice.

"Yes, yes… fine, I promise."

After this bit of appeasement Del seemed more at ease. So she began to recount, from the beginning, her stay at Greyford: about Meris and the window room, about Faron, the evil king who had usurped his brother's throne, and the prince, Corwan, who was to be put on trial in less than a week's time, and who would almost certainly be given a false trial, that is unless she were able to stop it.

Throughout all this, Mattie sat politely for the greater part of the hour, taking in every word. In the end, the two sat confounded, staring at the other girls playing around the yard. It was getting late. The warden would have someone out to ring the bell soon.

At last Mattie spoke up. "You're serious right? Not pulling my leg are you?"

"No. Honest," Del replied. Her head still full of worry and concern, so she rested her face back in her hands.

"What am I going to do?" Del repeated to herself.

And Mattie, who had come to sit down beside her during her story could clearly hear these words. At this moment, Del looked as if she hadn't a friend in the world; and it was for this reason that it then occurred to Mattie that she must instantly make a difficult decision. And consequently, if she were to choose to trust Delany, and her crazy stories, she would not be able to just stop there.

"What are *you* going to do? What are *we* going to do is more like it," she answered back.

Del sat astonished. "You're fooling..."

"Never," Mattie said, still trying to gain her determination. "The way I see it is you're likely to be caught, or killed, if you try going back there alone. You'll need my help, and you don't really have a choice about it."

She was insistent by now, and she was right. Del knew she was right. At this point, it appeared she had no other option but to accept Mattie's help.

The bell rang.

"Thank you..." Del said clutching her breath, yet still loud enough so that Mattie could plainly hear her, even above the sound of the bell.

CHAPTER FOURTEEN

IN THE MOONLIGHT

L ate the following evening, by the light of a nearly full moon, a dark hooded figure could be seen darting between the stone columns of the courtyard. That is to say, she would have been seen, most certainly seen, if anyone had been awake to notice her. Thankfully no one had.

At the end of the courtyard she paused to check behind her, before rushing off down the duskily lit path, and running slightly uphill, toward an old mysterious manor that looked grey in the moonlight.

This hooded figure was, of course, Mattie Hardy, as anyone could tell by the floundering way in which she snuck through the open night. Mattie had never been one for sneaking. In fact, this was very well the first time she could remember purposefully doing something wrong in a good long while, and certainly the first time she'd ever broken a rule while at Mayfield.

But there was no use in being careful about that now. She was on her way to save a prince, a kingdom, and something like a talking badger, if she'd understood correctly. To her conscience, it seemed only right to break curfew in one world, given that she was on her way to save a life in another.

Mattie could hear her breath as she hurried down the path. She could see icy wisps of it pass by in the night, and a long forgotten house was coming up quickly to meet her. In a few short steps she made it through the yard, and up the uneven front porch stairs.

Knock! Then creaking, the door opened almost immediately. And there was Del, wearing a disguise, something she'd found at the beginning of her stay at Greyford while searching through an old clothes chest, a rough peasantish robe belted around the waist. And draped across her arm was an extra robe for Mattie.

"I was beginning to worry," she said.

"Sorry. I had to wait till it was safe, for sure safe."

By this Mattie meant, more specifically, that she had been kept in her room by the precarious non-sleeping habits of her bunkmate, Margaret Thudman, who was a profound tattler. And incidentally, there were many near misses and false snorings exchanged before Mattie was able to make it safely from her room that night.

"Are you sure you're ready for this?"

Del had asked this for mainly two reasons: For one, because it was clearly told by her face, that Hardy, although resolute in her heart, was scared to death at the thought of what they were about to do. And secondly, because Del hadn't yet realized how afraid she herself was.

Mattie had stopped in the entryway to consider her answer. "Well, that's not really the point, is it?" she said at last, taking up the extra robe Del had found for her: and a deep, anxious breath.

CHAPTER FIFTEEN

WOULD-BE TRAVELERS

"**N**o. I don't think that's how it works," Mattie insisted.

To the reader: Some portions of this next chapter will contain various scientific concepts (i.e. eggheaded jargon), that you should feel at liberty to skim across, or skip entirely if you do not happen to care for that sort of thing. Still, I would chance a guess that there are some who will undoubtedly find this humdrum scholastic material to be quite intriguing. And so it is for those few, and for this reason, that I have decided to make mention of it here within the text. Granted, for those of us, myself included, who tend to fall somewhere in between the range of "liking science" and "disliking science", I've provided footnotes to explain some of the more difficult concepts.

Thus the two would-be travelers had gotten somewhat behind schedule, and at odds with each other regarding the processes and complexities involved in the act of returning to a previously visited planet, but at a different date and time[a].

Del had wrongly suggested that if the settings on the globe had worked on a previous occasion, then they

---

a   Why this should matter you will find out shortly, but it has something to do with a planet's orbital pattern.

should, ('obviously,' she said) work again. However, Mattie (who was right, and who had consequently paid better attention during science course) suggested that since planets, like everything in space, were always moving around, then they had better adjust the dials and coordinates, or run the risk of shooting at something that was no longer there and then who knows where they'd end up.

"See. Here it is," Mattie said, pointing to the open page of an enormous leather-bound ledger. (This was, indeed, that same book of charts Meris referenced before their last journey.) The book's age worn pages resembled that of an almanac[b], and it was hand written in thick black ink, with the name of a planet in bold script atop the page. It read:

Gleomu (catalogue # NX-147-T)

On the adjacent page, Mattie quickly found the day's date, December 10th, and began reciting a complicated series of numbers and angles to Del, who was adjusting the dials accordingly. This process took several minutes, and needed to be double checked often.

"I think this is it," Del said at last, flipping a switch she had seen Meris throw the day before. In a blink, the painting, which until then was merely dimly glowing rays of starlight into the room, burst out in a flash of color. The charts and maps Del had seen previously, realigned across it, and the scenes depicting the cities and valleys of Gleomu shone with renewed glory.

"I've never seen anything like it..." Mattie gasped.

However Del was still preoccupied about the globe.

---

[b] An Almanac is a detailed calendar of numbers and figures. In this case, it predicted the positioning of distant planets in relation to our own.

"What are these for?" she asked, pointing at the controls.

"I don't know. They probably mean something, right?" Mattie answered.

The two stood considering a set of three dials that had remained unturned.

"Oh. I've got it," Del finally exclaimed. "This one here is for minutes. See it goes up to 60," she said excitedly. "And that means this one's hours and… [giving a brief pause] this one's for days."

Del had given a pause, not because she was unsure of what the last dial represented, but rather, because she had noticed the upper limit numbered onto the dial, 365[ç]. Meaning that, if one wished it, they might spend a year, at most, stuck inside a far away world. She was glad she hadn't unknowingly adjusted this.

In the end, both agreed, considering they were likely to only get one try at this, to set it for the maximum that they could, and since all of Mayfield had the weekend off that meant two days; with the hope that, in the meantime, Mattie's roommate wouldn't go searching for her.

It was decided. So with all her strength Del began to turn the crank. Light grew in the room. This was no longer just an adventure.

[ç]   In actuality, this dial numbered up to 364, yet in the text above I wrote it as 365, in order not to confuse people. But since you have decided to read the explanation you may find this interesting. That the upper limit for full days was 364, as I had previously mentioned, and likewise the limit for hours was 23, and the minutes were numbered up to 60. So that when each dial was turned to its maximum, the total sum of each would equal 365 days.

CHAPTER SIXTEEN
HOW THEY CAME TO GLEOMU

At the start, you should remember that, until this last week, Del had never before used a globe for traveling. And also that, when she was first in Gleomu, she had noticed the city was built near a wide peaceful lake.

So that as the morning sun drew above the mountain peaks, their golden orb, obscured by the rays, glided down across the water. Going ever slower and getting closer to the calm waves, it stopped, unfortunately, some hundred feet from the shore. Then all at once, their light gave way, and the girls were dropped, with enough time to give a half scream before they hit the chilled water below.

The robes they had chosen to wear for disguises were soaked and weighed them down, and their heavy shoes made it difficult to tread water.

"Nicely done, Calbefur!" yelled Mattie, just able to keep her chin above the surface.

"It's not my fault!" Del answered. Although it technically had been.

So in like manner, soaked and mad about it, the pair kicked and paddled towards the shoreline, then collapsed onto the dirty bank: coughing, irritatingly cold, but they were not alone.

"Came all this way for a bath have you?" said a voice, from above them, and joking somewhat at their miserable bad luck.

Del turned to see a rough looking man with shoulder length hair standing behind them on the bank. Beyond him there roasted a low camp fire, and the warm smell of bread being baked in a pan. This gruff man found such amusement at their state. So much so, that Del had narrowly made up her mind to dislike him, that was before he spoke up again.

"Welcome, little ones. You can come warm up by the fire if you'd like," he said.

No one had ever called her a "little one" before, and Del didn't much prefer it. Yet the thought of being dried by the fire was enough to send both girls scrambling to their feet, and as close to the flames and smoke as they could bear. Del set out her stiff hands above the heat, while Mattie wrung out the wet corners of her robe.

After a while, when they were mostly dry, their host offered them a seat, a coarse blanket they had to share between them, and a light breakfast of wheat cakes made from the pan, washed down with a hot drink that tasted like ginger.

Through this whole time, however, not much was spoken, except for polite hospitalities, and a few over-adorned thank-yous that the girls had been dolefully forced to repeat while at Mayfield, yet here they were honestly meant. But so it was, that once both had been warmed and fed, at last their host spoke up. His voice was sturdy and, Del thought, a bit grandfatherly, but not the sort you'd like to hear if you'd been in trouble.

"I know who you are," he spoke.

The two girls froze in their seats, giving each other a quick look, terrified at what he might say next.

"Or more like it," he continued. "I can tell, within two guesses, which one of you was imprisoned in the king's palace about this time yesterday morn."

"How can you tell that?" and, "We don't know what you're talking about," were their responses.

(Unfortunately, both girls spoke over each other, interrupting one another. Del attempted to be sly about the whole thing, but Mattie, however, succeeded in ruining their chances for that.)

The old man seemed amused by this, as he sat tending the fire. Then after a space of time, he turned to answer Mattie's question, which she'd nearly forgot she'd asked.

"Child," he remarked, "It's not a subtle thing to break apart the king's dungeon. I'd dare say there's not a babe east of Theydor [a prominent river in the area] who hasn't heard of it by now." He laid a can of water on top of the coals to bring his tea to a boil. "And as for how I can tell you're the girl from those stories," he said, turning his glance towards Del, who looked away as soon as he did so. "You two have chosen an oddly cold spring morning to go out swimming. [the corners of his mouth started to grin] Yet somehow, you'd ended up in the middle of the lake, and that in full dress, without first kicking off your boots."

Del looked down at their wet laced shoes.

"...and I find that a little strange, don't you?" he added, stirring his drink to the soft sound of boiling water.

They'd been found out, undeniably so. Del's face made a grimace. For although she'd quite often had a knack for getting herself out of trouble, she knew that this time there was no getting around it.

(However, in all of this, there was a spot of good news that no one seemed to have realized, none except perhaps the old man. That since he hadn't noticed them glide down across the lake that morning, being so close to where they'd landed, it could be reasonably assumed, then, that no one else would have: except that this was not entirely true, either. As it happened, there had been yet one other person who'd seen their glittering, golden orb, floating down through the clouds that morning, and that person being a little girl who'd lived just outside the city gates with her mother. Who would, at the first light of dawn every morning, go down to the lake to fetch some water. Howbeit this morning, she'd been so overwhelmed by what she'd seen that she left her buckets. And went running back along the path to tell her mother, who, in turn, chided her for not keeping up with her chores.)

"Do you mean to turn us in?" Del asked, after a long silence.

"What do you think?" he said, sipping his tea. "Would I have fed you breakfast, if I'd meant to turn you in?"

She thought about that for a second.

"No… I don't think so," she said at last, desperately hoping she was right about it.

"No," he reassured her. "Not to mention that also, at the moment, I myself would be, as well, all too welcomed by the palace guards."

This last statement was somewhat confusing, but Mattie thought she knew what was meant by it. "So you're a fugitive, then?" she asked, a little excited to have said the words.

He took out the pan from the fire, and began to mix in grain for his late breakfast. "Some... the criminals more likely, would say that, but by those who'd know better I should assume they'd think of me as a hero."

Del would have never guessed him to be a fugitive. So she broke in, asking a very obvious question. "I don't understand," she said. "If you're trying to run away, then why are you camped out here, so close to the city?"

For indeed, they were not so close to the city as to be seen easily by the guards along the tower, but certainly, as Del knew enough about military things to know, that even a half-decent search party could find a lone man not more than five miles from their own gate.

"Who said I was running away?" he replied. "I'm a fugitive, yes, but I've no intention of running away. Faron..." he pressed on, in full voice, perhaps still a bit irritated at the thought that he might be running away, "is an evil king, I'll give you that, but he's lazy, and the thugs he's hired are just like him. Every morning, after the sun's risen nearly a hand's breadth above the hills, they leave the gates and head out riding west [pointing out across the plains], so as to not have to ride with a glare in their eyes. And after a long while their route comes about, and they'll end up crossing this side of the lake at around dusk. You see, even an old man like myself can outwit a bunch of blithering oafs, if not but for fifteen minutes a day."

At the end of this, the old man went back again to his unattended breakfast, and Del was not in the mood to ask any further questions. Though Mattie, on the other hand, was still quite curious. And she proceeded to ask him, in a similar way, what he'd done to warrant such enmity from the king.

To this, the old man answered her plainly that good men have for always been the natural enemies of tyrants.

Yet this, still, would not suffice Mattie's curiosity, and so he began to retell a very elaborate and interesting story, between sips of tea and morsels of bread. Beginning first with his rise to prominence within the ranks of the royal army, and then the sudden and suspicious death of the true king, along with Faron's disbandment of the King's forces, and lastly (and what both girls thought to be most interesting) his cunning escape from the city, and from Faron's ever widening grasp, by a bit of distraction and a well-timed horse cart.

As you might imagine, reader, this was a very involved story and took the old man a good deal of time to explain fully. Therefore, I will not belabor you with the details of it, for they are many. Except that to say what some may have already guessed at, that their present storyteller was, in fact, the last surviving general of the late King Reuel: a General Gamel, as his soldiers would address him, but the girls seemed to favor calling him "Gam".

CHAPTER SEVENTEEN

TO THE CITY

I n case you were wondering from the previous
chapter, whether or not Del had ever mentioned to
Gamel about her conversation with Corwan, or about
Meris and her escape from the king's prison, or about their
hopes to somehow rescue the prince before his trial, the
truth is she had. But Gamel, who was not all that fond of
relying on the girls' "magic", as he called it, said they'd be
better served to wait until Corwan was released from
prison, on the day of his trial. And that if they'd attempt to
storm the castle before then, that even if by chance they
were successful, Faron, who'd been looking for any
opportunity he could to slay the boy, would undoubtedly
order his execution during the commotion, and then all
their effort would have been for naught.

They did however come to a conclusion, during a lunch
of pan fried trout and wild yam, that they might be able to
properly manage a rescue for Meris from the palace
gardens: Which was not too heavily guarded, at the
present time, and may easily be gotten into by cover of
darkness, but saying that they would first need to get into
the city.

The daylight was falling down below the plains to the
west. Gamel ordered the girls to the task of concealing
any signs of their fire. Most of the coals were gathered
and thrown into the lake, while he took great care to be

sure every footprint was swept way. Towards dusk, he led them through a thicket, to a hidden hollowed tree. He told them they could sleep there till he'd come again later that evening.

"This is the most uncomfortable place in the world..." Mattie remarked, although she was soon fast asleep, and slept more soundly than Del did that night.

It was completely dark. There was a rattling in the bushes. Del awoke quickly, and for a moment forgot where she was. Shaking and stirring, the noise grew louder, till at once the bushes were pulled back. A little light came in.

"It's time," a voice said. [This was Gamel's voice]

"What time is it?" Mattie asked in a yawn, for she had just woken up.

The moon was not full like it had been in our world. Most often Del would only know to duck, because she kept her hands out to feel for her way. Too often, along the path, she'd kick a misplaced root or some hidden stone, and Del would have thought it impossible to continue on in these conditions, except that Gam seemed unaffected by the darkness. "*Perhaps he has gone this way before,*" she thought.

It was not long till their uncomfortable winding trail finally broke from the heavy wood. It led them onward, through tall grasses. Up ahead the city (which you should know is named Ismere) was mostly dark, that they could see, save for a few torches along the watchtowers.

No words were spoken. Del followed cautiously behind Gamel, and Mattie behind her. She wondered how they would ever get into the city without being seen, and she rightfully decided that this was either the bravest thing she'd ever done, or the most foolhardy, and that it was still too early to tell which it might be. The towered walls rose to meet them. Del pressed her palms against the massive quarried stone, still warmed from the day's sun.

Then there was a whistling sound like a bird's song. Cupping his hands to his lips, Gamel made a sound that almost none but the keenest watchman would suspect. Then suddenly, a rope was thrown down from atop the battlement, its tip reaching the ground only a few feet from where they stood. The general gave a tug to be sure it was securely fastened.

When he was satisfied with this, Gamel turned back to the girls, and in a hushed voice he said, "You see… we still have many friends in hiding. Faron may well kill the shepherds, but he cannot scatter their sheep." (This he said regarding the fallen generals and their armies.)

In the dark and shadows, within a minute, both girls were given a crash course in the simple mechanics of wall scaling. And Del, being the stronger of the two, was encouraged to go first, followed there after by Mattie, and then by Gamel, who would wait till last in case either fell.

"And remember," he whispered. "Be as silent as you can, even if you feel yourself about to fall."

There was no going back. Del grabbed at the rope, and on her second try began to walk her feet out in front of her. Her arms ached. Her hands were red and sore, though she wasn't yet halfway up the wall.

"*I can't give up. I can't...*" she repeated with every new step. All the muscles in her limbs spiked with pain. The next step. Her hands were now blistering. The next step.

At the brim, she was very near screaming. Till suddenly a strong hand grabbed her by her feeble arms, and pulled her swiftly onto the ledge. The great stones of the city wall felt cold now. She was deathly tired, and lay there till Mattie and Gam had both made it safely up the wall together, being that Mattie wasn't strong enough to make it up on her own.

The city of Ismere was sparsely lit. Its streets were dreaming below them. And soon, before she was quite ready, they were up again. The dark figure who'd pulled Delany to safety led them down the darkest alleyways, between closed shops, through the narrowest avenues, and into a low door.

In the corner of a spare room, Del and Mattie were offered a makeshift bed of cushions, which they graciously accepted, for by then it was very late. Also, they were helplessly tired. So no fuss was made about sharing a bed, nor about the coarseness of their pillows. And they were soon fast asleep, again.

CHAPTER EIGHTEEN
OF NEW PLANS AND OLD MEN

T he next morning, a panel of light shot out from between the wood-slatted shutters. It warmed Del's cheek and shone into one of her eyes. Truthfully though, this beam had been creeping along the floor since sunrise, for by now it was nearly noon.

Del squinted her eyes, trying to rub the glare out of them. She felt along the bed, but Mattie wasn't there. (Mattie awoke much earlier that morning, having slept far better, on both occasions, than Del had the previous evening.) But just then, from the kitchen, came a noise that could not have been mistaken for anything else, a kiddish sort of laugh.

Through the open entryway, Del could now hear bursts of excited, hearty laughter. Uninterested, she rolled about for a few minutes, trying her hardest to fall back asleep. But as most might find, under similar circumstance, she could not. Her body still ached from climbing the night before, which made her forearms smart as she sat up in bed. And then, as if to speak above the noise of laughter, she heard a loud, unfamiliar voice saying:

" ...and remember the time we all rode out to Lochshire for May Festival?" Here the two men broke out, once more, in roaring laughter, Gamel apparently knowing already what the man was about to say, as if he had heard it told many times before. Del was now standing in the doorway and could see the two men sitting at opposite ends of a square table, and Mattie in between, sipping tea, fully amused by the old men and their stories. Then the other man, turning to Mattie, who could not stop grinning, continued his story. (Good reader, to better understand his story you should note that a crest is a common currency in that territory of Gleomu, roughly the equivalent of one British pound.)

"You see, deary," he said, "Gamel had convinced us, said we'd each save two crests each if we'd just agree to a week's sleep out in the fields."

Here Gamel interrupted, "And we did, as I recall," he said pointing to his chest. "Fourteen crests in all, between the seven of us, it was..."

"Sure, sure," the other man conceded. And turning again to Mattie, "Yes, but every morning we'd have the shepherds' sheep grazing near our heads."

Mattie giggled, trying to cover up the bite of toast in her mouth.

"And what harm did it do you?" Gamel exclaimed.

"Ha! Except for a blasted fear of farm animals, I cannot tell," he said, and laughed roaringly.

At this point, the lively group noticed Del standing there and offered her a warm cup of tea, and a bread roll with jam. The stocky storyteller at the table was indeed the same dark figure from the night before. This man, Radcliffe, was as you may have gathered, a long-time friend of Gamel's, since childhood. (And also, it should be noted, he'd served as a lieutenant general under Gamel during the great war. Yet, through all this, they had still remained friends.)

From here on, the rest of the day seemed oddly routine, considering the dangerous plans they were to attempt that night. Around noon, Radcliffe's wife, Rhoda, returned from market with a cart of ham and vegetables to make for supper, and some other pastries and sweet cake she had got for them all. At this, Radcliffe was a bit upset. For although he loved sweet cakes more than most, he said she should have avoided raising suspicions.

She only laughed at his cautions, however, "If they've not suspected us by now, with all the food I buy for us, I daren't say they'd pay us any mind for a few extra cakes."

The city streets were quiet again that evening. So that by cover of darkness, when it was well into the later watches of the night, the three fugitives left out the back door of the house, and scurried in among the dimly lit alleys. It was previously decided, over a hefty supper, that there would be no use for Radcliffe to join in with them this time, seeing as four are more easily spotted than three, and also because they hadn't needed his help to get into the palace.

Yet, during their meal that evening, the men, using a stir of military phrases which neither of the girls had understood, not even Del (who may have had a good chance at it, considering she'd grown-up around such talk); The men agreed that Radcliffe was to follow not too far behind, carrying a torch and an empty water pitcher he was to fill at the fountain in the main square. The strategic reasoning for these being, of course, that the torchlight might serve to flush out any of the king's spies, and also, that the empty water pitcher would give him an adequate excuse for wandering about the city streets at night.

Del could hardly see her steps in the midnight around her. They trailed through the darkest, most obscure parts of the city toward the rear of the palace, and they were all completely silent, though the girls' hard-soled shoes made a subtle tapping as they ran from shadow to shadow. In one instance, they were nearly seen by a baker as he set out in the very early morning hours for work.

The streets led uphill, then wound up to a high wall, but only about a fourth as tall as the one they had climbed the night before.

"Is there no other way in?" Mattie asked, trying to sound exhausted, but Gamel refused to answer. She had been dreading this next part of the mission ever since she'd heard about it, but there was no other way in, and she would have to climb over the wall alone.

"Very well..." she said below her breath, as she was hoisted up to stand upon Del's shoulders, who was then made to stand on Gamel's shoulders.

Mattie's breath shortened. She braced herself frantically against the wall. This was not the sort of thing she'd naturally been accustomed to. She stood on her toes, but it was still not enough.

"A little more," she softly called down below.

"Oh, come on, Hardy. You can do it," Del urged, trying to keep a good attitude about it.

"I can't though," Mattie said, for the top was still several feet above her head. Mattie stretched the tips of her fingers as far as they could go, but it was still no use.

"Hold on now," came Gam's voice from below as he grabbed at Del's feet and, with a strain, lifted them both up, his hands now above his head.

At last, it was just enough. Mattie grabbed at the top and squirmed her way onto the rim of the wall. Below her lay the dark stillness, the palace gardens with its rows of hedges. Within a moment Mattie was down the other side, using the slack end of a rope Gamel had thrown up to her.

Her feet touched down onto the cushy garden sod. The hedges loomed, too high to be seen over. To her left the corridor wound in through the dark like a maze, and to her right it was the same. Neither route, she thought, looked particularly promising, and then it hit her. She knew where she was, or better yet to say in what she was, having before read books about this sort of thing.

"*Not now,*" she thought. Then saying the words out loud, although she hadn't meant to, "...a labyrinth."

CHAPTER NINETEEN

LOST

L ost. Mattie Hardy was hopelessly lost. As she walked hesitantly around corners and seemingly endless passages, this thought pervaded her senses. It made her breath dry and shaky, until at last it was unavoidable. She was altogether completely unfound.

To her credit though, at the out start, she had tried to do a rather sensible thing. From the stories she'd read, she knew the smart thing to do when you're trapped inside a labyrinth is to leave a trail for yourself, and at that she gave a good attempt, by unraveling the rope that she'd climbed down the wall with along her path. Yet, several paces and turns ago she'd run out of rope, though not out of maze. Even still, what made matters worse was that the night was in its darkest hours, after the moon has set and while the stars are dimmed.

A split up ahead. She chose left, although she might have just as likely chose right. Both paths were now obscured by deep shadows, and no path seemed separate from the other. She was lost, and so continued on.

Though, after some bit of lostness, the hedges were not so black looking as they had been before. She could see a tinge of the faintest green in them, and her footsteps were not so hidden as they had once been.

"*Hurry!*" she thought, for she knew that time was getting away from her. From deep inside she wanted to scream out for help, but knew she shouldn't. That would give herself away for sure.

Her lips moved now, and what may have been intended as an idea, came out as a whisper.

"Help me..." she spoke out, softly in the still night air. Though, be as it may, she did not know the reason why she'd said this aloud, nor to whom she may have been speaking.

Likely some may argue that what occurred next may be merely an instance of probability, not at all related to Mattie's frail pleading found within the previous paragraph. Notwithstanding, I would rather choose the side that would think these two related, given how often miracles are mistaken for common luck, and vice versa.

Thusly, however remarkable this may have been, Mattie, from this point onward, found her way through the maze with growing ease. After a series of four consecutive proper turns, the corridor led out to an iron gate and a well trimmed lawn, and the sleeping palace beyond that.

"Meris..." Mattie hushed from inside the gate.

"Meris," she said again. Still there was no response. The palace lawn was harshly silent.

"Meris," she repeated, only much louder than before, not wanting to venture outside the labyrinth gates for fear of being spotted in the growing daylight. Then, at once, there arose a motion from the bushes to her left, and out waddled a noticeably chubby creature with greying whiskers.

"Dear me... I heard you the first time. No need to go on shout'n and wake the guards. I was wondering when you'd- Oh."

He stopped short when he realized the girl inside the gate was not who he'd expected.

"Who are you?" he asked, quite rudely, but only because he was just woken up, and also because he was so surprised.

"Mattie," she said. "Delany and I came here to rescue you, but we need to hurry. It's almost day now."

The few clouds in the sky blushed with the golden morning rays.

"So it is," said Meris, looking up towards the horizon. "Well if we were in such a hurry, why didn't you say so sooner?"

Mattie wanted to defend herself, but knew that that would only take up more time. And so, hurrying, she motioned for Meris to follow her back through the labyrinth, meaning to use the rope she'd unwound along her path to help them get over the wall, but she was not being listened to. Apparently, her furry companion had already had plans of his own.

"This way then," the gopher exclaimed and was off, escaping across the lawn towards the far wall. Mattie followed as fast as her legs could move. In most cases, the pair would have been captured here, running through the palace grounds in the early morning hours, but, as you may remember, Faron's hired guards were all terribly lazy, so there was little chance any would be awake so soon.

The little mammal ran at top speed, ducking into a thick set of bushes. Their branches scraped against Mattie's cheeks.

"Here it is."

He pointed to a wide hole near the edge of the wall.

"Down this way," he said, and leapt headlong into the black earth. As you can imagine this was an unpleasant sight.

"Do I have to?" Mattie protested.

His even-toned face and dirtied paws stuck up from below the ground. "Yes," he replied.

His head quickly disappeared again, and then he added, with the echo of the tunnel around him, "You'll like it."

CHAPTER TWENTY

DARK AND LIGHT

Nothing could be seen. It was absolute darkness. All Mattie knew was the sound in front of her to lead the way and the grimy earth that enclosed her. She most certainly did not *like it*. Her only solace, then, were in thoughts of what the high society back home would have to say about such a thing, and how their noses curled up at the mere mention of dirt.

Up ahead the tunnel thinned, so that she had to almost go crawling on her belly to get by. Before her, she heard Meris heaving and straining at some large weight that blocked their exit. Then the stone gave way, and it bathed the tunnel in swelling light. Meris sprung from the darkness, followed closely by Mattie, squeezing her head and shoulders through the opening.

All around her was blindness. There was a considerable commotion and, by the sound of it, horse hooves and rolling carts. She knew at once, they had dug up through the waking city streets.

"*Eeehh!*" cried an old woman by the side of the road.

"What now?" yelled the deep voice of a man, who was now trying, unsuccessfully, to calm the fears of his aging cart horse.

Her eyes were adjusting. A small crowd was quickly gathering round to see the girl who'd crawled up through the street. She was stunned.

"Come on," Meris pulled at her sleeve.

This woke her. In a second she was out of the hole, and sprinting through the lane, back along the wall to where she'd first begun that night. But as they bent around the last corner it was plain to see, things outside the wall were not going so well either.

Several gruff and mean characters, some with sticks, had backed Del and Gamel into the entryway of a locked house that faced out towards the lane.

"Now, now... let's not have any trouble," their leader smirked.

Defiantly, Del grabbed at a stone along the ground, and hurled it towards one of the hoodlums closest to her, but he narrowly dodged it.

"Watch it, love. Don't make this any harder than it ought to be," he issued.

The air around Del's face lightened, and the man she'd narrowly missed came at her quickly, holding his stick higher in his hand.

"This'll teach you," he muttered.

What happened next was like a blur. Meris, who had not stopped running since they'd left the tunnel, shot out with full force into the crowd, and threw himself onto the man's thigh, biting as hard as he could.

"*Ahkk!*"

The thug let out a terrible scream, and this was the perfect opportunity. In a flash, Gamel had the man's stick out of his hand, and the two others nearest to him lay whimpering on the ground. Though in all this scuffle, Del was knocked off her feet.

"Are you alright?" Mattie caught up and knelt there beside her.

"I'm fine," she replied, holding her head, and her eyes squinting tightly. "Do you hear that awful ringing though?"

To this Mattie gave a mothering smile.

"You must have hit your head harder than you thought-" But while she said this, she went to place her hand onto Del's forehead, in an attempt to console her, but was instantly startled by something she'd never have expected.

"Oh!" Mattie cried.

"What is it?"

"That ringing. I hear it too now."

And this ringing grew like a thunder. Light burst forth around them now like the birth of a star.

"Quickly, Meris. Hurry!" Del shouted, much louder than she knew, because of the immensity of the sound in her ears.

Meris, however, had not heard any such noise at all, for it had confined itself in a way that only the girls could hear it. Still, he knew immediately what it was, once he saw the panicked look on their faces, and he left the fight to run and join in with them, but it was too late.

A strong barrier had now formed between them. He pressed his paws against the golden light in vain. On the inside, Del put her hands opposite his.

"I'm so sorry," she said, starting to tear, but he could not hear her. His eyes looked distracted, beyond hers, to a new crowd of men who had just then realized what was happening; After seeing the explosion of light, and the orb forming around the girls, they were running out to try their claim at the king's reward money, if any were still to be had.

At this sight, Gamel threw down the stick he'd managed to steal away from one of the thugs. And then, yelling something inaudible to Meris the two turned about, and ran as fast as their legs enabled them to, down the lane away from the main square.

This was the last Del saw then. For at that moment, they were shot up toward the heavens, leaving behind an awestruck and bewildered mob.

CHAPTER TWENTY-ONE

A FOUL GAME

"We didn't do much good with it, did we?" Del finally spoke up.

The two had been sitting blankly for some while during recreation hour that next morning. It was otherwise cheerful in the yard, though. Governor Hanessy had organized an exhibition match against a rival girls' school from Sussex, but both girls were withheld to the sidelines.

The reasons for this being: For Mattie, that although she was indeed a remarkable bowler (having been forced into private lessons every summer since the beginning of primary school), she was unfortunately never allowed the opportunity to show it while at Mayfield; And, by my judgement, I think the underlying reason why she did not protest much about the fact was that, in her heart, she was never all that fond of cricket to begin with. For Del, it was that for a long time that morning she'd complained about not feeling well. (Which was, to some extent, true.)

"Do you think they made it out alright?" Mattie asked.

"Oh, I don't know..." Del answered, shuffling her feet aimlessly. "We can't know for sure till we get back."

"You want to go back there?" Mattie said hesitantly.

"Sure. Don't you?"

"Well... yes, but I can't see what good we'll do. We can't get into the city by ourselves, and even if we did we'd never make it into the palace."

Mattie had let her eyes wander down as she said these words, for she knew by now that she should have been braver than this.

But before Mattie could completely finish these words, however, Del's face began to flash a tempered red. She'd indignantly wished to call Hardy all sorts of awful names for wanting to back out on their duties now, not the least of which was a "coward".

Del clenched both fists tightly.

"Oh, don't be so selfish, Hardy!" she said.

But Mattie, now sounding all too much like her father (who would often say such things)[3], she retaliated, "I'm not being *selfish*... just being smart about it is all."

Del drew in her bottom lip, to hold in her tongue. "Yeah, well they're the same thing sometimes," she said.

In response to this, Mattie said not a word, but kept her stare towards the ground. Out in the yard, the morning's skirmish against Sussex was not going so well either. So that even the most typically hopeful spectators were noticeably starting to lose their muster. Mattie knew the feeling.

"Please come back with me," Del finally spoke up. "I've got no chance at all if you're not there."

---

[3] As you might like to know, Mattie's father had made a name for himself, during the war, as an author of protest literature. So that in her younger years, Mattie would often find herself repeating some of her father's pacifist slogans as a reflex, until she had come to establish her own thoughts on the matter.

Mattie thought, and let out a deep sigh, becoming more like herself as she did. "Alright," she said, looking back up, and smiling for the first time that day.

(Now, if you may remember, until this point both girls had not been truly friends, not in any lasting way that is. It was only that they had just recently, and painfully, forsaken enemyship, and were only just beginning the first processes of friendhood, which was now coming into fruition; And it was here, at this memory, that I believe both girls would recount as their true beginning.)

Del smiled back, a very genuine smile. For she knew no matter what, that from here on they would be in this together.

That night Del had a horrible time sleeping. Her bed was far more comfortable than anything she'd had in days, but her mind was far too turbulent for resting. They needed some heroic plan before tomorrow night, and the Prince's trial. But, how would they ever get back into the palace now, unseen? - she thought. Though at last, she decided that this of course was impossible. Which left then, only one other option, and it was not a very good one.

CHAPTER TWENTY-TWO

IN THE DEEP PRISON

T he deep prison halls of Ismere were solemn that next evening. Prince Corwan sat upright against the back wall of his cell, his wrists and ankles clapped in irons. For since the king had already needed to deal with the mysterious losses of two fugitive prisoners so far this week, and would have no more such instances, "...that might smear the good name of the crown," as he put it, he therefore commanded that Corwan be relocated to the bottommost chamber of his dungeon, to be locked securely in chains, awaiting his summons to court at sunrise.

Tomorrow's "trial", if it could be called that in good conscience, would almost certainly be rigged against his favor, but there was no other way. And the council, as of late, as his brother Reuel would often complain, "...is becoming increasingly overrun by lesser men." Sadly, Corwan knew there was little hope for him now, because of this. Most would fall to Faron's army, and those who could not be pressured would be bought. Thus leaving the worthy few that remained faithful to the crown too inconsequential to raise a sufficient vote. All this he knew, through logic. "*But perhaps,*" he hoped, "*a rescue might come by some other means.*"

It was late on the eve of his supposed execution. There was a frantic weariness in his mind that would not be subdued by worry, and his arms ached because of the chains. Thus, after a few more similar thoughts, his eyes began to sag. Then, weighed down by the heaviness of these thoughts, he put his head back and fell asleep, but this was not to last for long.

Soon after, the prince awoke to a grating, scratching, peculiar sort of sound coming from the darkened corner of his cell. The unsuspectedness of which startled him (as I believe it would most). It was odd though, in the sense that it did not appear to be coming from within the room at all, but from below rather, as if the world's largest mole were ascending up through the depths to meet him. This burrowing, which began as a hardly distinguishable ticking sound, grew more audible every second. Till at last it burst from the ground in the shadowed corner of the room, letting out a distinctly human-like sigh.

Corwan sat back further against the wall when he heard it speak. From the blackened shadows of his cell he could hear a whisper: a very hushed, earthy whisper. His ears strained to hear what it said.

"Eh there... you the prince?" the voice spoke.

"Is someone there?" Corwan quietly and cautiously replied, so as to not wake the guards who sat outside his door.

This irritated the voice. Who then answered back, not so delicately as before, "Of course there's someone here. I asked you a question, didn't I?"

"Yes, well... you might have been my imagination, so that's why I asked," he said, squinting in the dark to see whom he might be speaking with.

"Oh, come on. You haven't gone mad yet, have you? Haven't even been in here that long," the voice said.

"Yes, well I do see your point," Corwan answered, "but then again it is the middle of the night, and you did just crawl up through my floor."

The creature chuckled, "*Ha.* You could jolly well make anything sound crazy if you'd say it like that."

"Indeed..." the prince agreed hesitantly. Though not yet completely at ease, being unable to discern his intruder, but he having a clear view of him in fettered chains. So shorty after this, Corwan asked the thing politely, if it wouldn't mind stepping out into the lighted portion of the room. To which it eagerly obliged, saying at once that it had "forgotten its manners" and also that His Majesty ought to try to "keep his head on him" and "keep a tight lip", so that they wouldn't have any trouble and accidentally wake the guards.

All this was of course fine by the prince, who'd agreed to stay calm, so long as the voice did nothing hostile. This took only one or two moments to be agreed upon. So that in the end, out from the shadows emerged a dirty, furry-faced creature, thoroughly tired from a full day's worth of good digging. He waddled towards the prince, and was oddly at eye level to him as he approached. In an instant Corwan realized that this "person" to whom he had been speaking was in fact not a person at all, but (as you may have already guessed) Meris, who had been digging heroically, since mid-morning, trying to reach Corwan's cell before he was taken to trial at sunrise.

The chubby mammal stopped, several feet before the prisoner, in the silhouette of dim torchlight that came wafting in through the open hatch in the door.

"I'm here to rescue you," he said, and shook some of the lingering dust from his furry coat. His Majesty was perplexed, and rightly so.

"A gopher...?" he said.

CHAPTER TWENTY-THREE

ΛT THE GATES

"There's no way *on earth* we'll make it in there without being caught," Mattie warned.

The two girls were dressed again in their disguises, peering over the crest of a hill toward the city gates afar off. A raggedy old thorn bush in front of them blocked their clear view of the watchtower, but it needn't have bothered. They both knew that tower was there, and that this was a right foolhardy mission.

"You're right," Del said, affirmingly, as if she'd known this all along.

Mattie's eyes looked cross now. "Why do you say it like that?" she questioned. But Del paid her no attention, as she was already several paces ahead when Mattie said this. She had obviously not intended to stay in hiding.

"Was this your big idea? To have us captured?" Mattie yelled out in disbelief.

Del turned about, stopping for just one second, "Yes. Now come on."

"Ohhh..." Mattie quickly stood, and ran along after her to catch up. "All this space travel's gone to your head, Calbefur!" And when she was at last able to match Del's stride, she blurted out, "You knew I'd never have agreed to this."

If you can imagine sounding both compassionate and irritated all at the same time, then you will likely know how Del sounded in this moment.

"I'm sorry. I really am," she explained. "But this is the only way. Trust me, will you?"

Mattie sighed, a very loud sigh. "I sure hope you've thought this one through."

Del did not respond to this, however, because she was too busy wondering for herself whether or not she truly had thought this through all the way.

Ahead, Ismere was tensely chaotic that morning. A steady stream of rural farmers, and even some from the neighboring towns and villages could be seen forming a line at the main gate. One cart in particular, filled to the top with likely enthusiasts, came from as far away as Lochmead. (Which, in case you hadn't known, is typically a full two days journey from the capital by horseback, and suspectedly longer if you traveled by cart.) Most common folk, who could afford to do so, had taken the day off just so that they might be nearer to the morning's proceedings, awaiting news from the high council.

And so it was, in this manner, that Mattie and Del made their way to a position towards the back of the line. Those who stood before them looked to have mixed expressions. For the most part, their faces were mournful or solemn, though a few appeared to be nervously excited; and even one lanky fellow, at the head of the line, Del thought for sure looked strangely happy.

A short, fat man in a wide floppy hat, and a tall man with the longest white beard either girl had ever seen, stood huddled directly in front of them. They spoke in low voices about the state of the kingdom, and of this present situation. Mattie and Del strained their ears to hear what the men said, but gave careful attention to look about every so often, trying unsuccessfully to appear disinterested.

"I just don't see why more men won't stand up to him, is all," said the man in the wide hat.

"True, true, very well... but tell me, what are *you* doing about it, Mortimer?" asked the bearded man.

"Oh, come off it. You know I've got a weak heart," the large man vigorously answered back. Then in a lower voice, "Couldn't possibly do much good, you know."

"See, *there*... that's precisely my point," the tall man replied. "Nearly all men have weak hearts, in one way or another."

After this, the men's conversation drifted to matters of finance, specifically the new land tax the king had recently proposed to council and its implications on local sheep herders, which was a topic neither girl found particularly interesting.

(And I would assume, reader, that you would as well find the rest of their discussion tiresome, and much too adult-ish to be worth its ink. So then, if you'll permit me, I would like to go back now to Corwan, and an event that happened earlier that morning within the palace, while Del and Mattie were still busy examining the city gate, deciding whether or not to move forward with their mission.)

You see, earlier that morning, at sunrise, when the jailor came to collect the prince for his well anticipated trial, he found the prisoner's cell just as he had left it and Corwan patiently seated, still in chains, showing no signs of struggle.

But why had he not taken his opportunity to escape, you may be wondering? Well, there were multiple reasons for this: One being that, while although it may have been technically possible to break the prince free from his chains, the entire process would likely have caused such a clatter that they could never have completed it in time to escape back down the tunnel, not without first being discovered by the guards who sat sleeping just outside his door.

Though this was, in fact, a secondary reason for why Corwan had not tried his hand at escaping. The main reason being this: He had come to the realization that he could not in good conscience succeed in escaping, and so it would be better then not to try.

(This seems a strange thing to say, but it is truth, as clearly as it's written.) Corwan knew the state of his kingdom: The fragile hearts of his forces now that their generals were (the honest ones at least) nearly all dead, or missing and rightfully presumed dead. What's more, he knew that any form of escaping would then require preparations for a civil war. And that, they would certainly lose, having no fortified city and neither the means with which to equip an army.

In addition, he knew the sweeping wrath of his brother's anger. And that he, Faron, had been uncharacteristically merciful to the old jailor in recent days, after Del's miraculous flight from the dungeon. Presumably because even Faron in his arrogance could grasp at how impossible it would be for any living person to forcibly constrain a prisoner who's able to break apart stone roofs like pieces of parchment.

So Corwan was led from the depths of the prison that morning, his hands still bound in front of him. And what of Meris you may ask? Well, he was sent back to Gamel in the early hours of dawn with a message from His Majesty, the Prince, and a new plan by which they might regain the throne.

And so then this brings us again to the front of the line, where the girls were both standing, nervously awaiting admittance into the city.

"Do you think anyone will recognize us?" Mattie whispered.

Del looked towards her friend and shrugged her shoulders, but would not answer Mattie in words for fear that her voice would betray her own rising nervousness.

When it was at last their turn to be checked by the guards for weapons, and to explain their business that day within the gates, Del did something so rash that even she felt the need to apologize to herself for having done it. As soon as they arrived at the front of the line she did not waste any time, but walked right on toward the head gatekeeper. And he was easy to spot, being that he was the only man seated, not going about his duties. His scraggly beard and fat torso folded in on itself as he reclined with his feet propped up, pretending to nap, his rickety chair titled back against the wall.

Del cleared her throat, primarily to garner his attention, though partially for her own benefit as well.

"Excuse me... ah, sir," she said.

He opened his puffy, wrinkled eyes.

"Huh," he grumbled. "What do you want, little girl?"

His voice was unappealing, but Del knew there was no going back on her decision now. So she inhaled a quick breath, and continued, "I, and my friend here," she said, pointing behind her, "have... have come to turn ourselves in."

"We've what?!" Mattie called out in astonishment.

"And also, I'm not a little girl," Delany added.

The slovenly gatekeeper sighed heavily, with his hands folded across his stomach, and his chair still tilted back against the gate wall. "Alright, little miss, alright. What is it then?" he said, trying a play as if he were already completely wearied by their conversation, and had many other better things to do. "You forget to do your chores this morning?" he asked, and rudely laughed at his perceived wit.

Del's faced winced, for she didn't prefer being treated like a child. "No," she said crossly, and a bit loudly. "We've murdered the King."

There was an audible gasp from those around. At once, all activity at the city gate ceased, and every eye turned to face hers. All were dramatically still, all except for the head gatekeeper that is, who was frantic, clumsily reaching around for the hilt of his sword, even quite before he could stand.

Mattie's face fell wide with disbelief.

"You're joking..." she muttered, as the guard closest to her grabbed at her arm. No matter what trouble they could have got into at Mayfield, this was now far worse.

CHAPTER TWENTY-FOUR

THE TRIAL

A ccording to law, Corwan was brought before the high council within the month of his accusing, to stand trial for the murder of his brother, King Reuel. The Court of Decrees, to where Corwan was brought that morning, was an ornately decorated meeting hall near the main square of the city. And that day, the main hall (which bears, coincidentally, a slight resemblance to the Court of Lords in London) flooded to overflowing.

Every living member of the high council was in attendance. And besides this, there stood crammed tightly together a sea of commoners around the edges of the room, and the very brutest of Faron's hired men were spread throughout, "...in order to keep the peace," as he said. Though from the look of it, they seemed rather like they were there more for the purposes of intimidation, than for reasons of peace.

Corwan stood in the center of it all. Yet presently, every eye and ear inclined itself to the words of a spidery-looking man who sat in a red plush chair before the council: giving his testimony, as it were. (This was that same lanky man Del had seen at the head of the line into the city, the man who'd looked strangely happy.) His fingers were pale and boney. And his dress was like that of a man who desires to impress people, yet doesn't truly have the right clothes for it.

"Yes, that's right," he spoke eloquently, with the S's of his words dragging on. "I heard him [the prince] say, on multiple occasions, how he was jealous of his brother's title and throne, and he wanted to take them for himself." The man's thin voice made you itch in your skin when you heard it.

"And he did tell you then, that he had plans to kill his brother, the King?" asked the court officiant in a loud assuming voice, being sure to articulately form each syllable so to be clearly heard by all.

"Sure..." The spidery-looking man's nose twitched and his eyes gleamed. "Even showed me the knife he planned to do it with," the witness said, grinning strangely.

At these words, the crowd erupted with boos and accusations, and the hall quickly swelled with the sounds of argument, as intermingled pockets of council members stood and began to hurl insults at one another. Corwan yelled, his face flushed red with anger. "Liar!" he cried, shaking his chains and pointing at the man.

"Silence!" Faron slammed his fist down repeatedly on the arm of the throne. "Silence!" he commanded.

When at last the room was quieted (and this took a good deal of time), the officiant spoke out again.

"May I remind the prisoner," he said, "that he should try to keep his anger under control." When the officiant said these words, his eyes gave a crooked glint, and his mouth a subtle smirk, though most were too far off to see it, but Corwan could see it.

The witness, a weaver by occupation, was then asked to plainly describe the knife that Corwan was alleged to have shown him. And his response was effortlessly masterful in its deception, full of false starts and stammers. So that it might seem as if he were actually remembering, instead of only pretending to remember. (And you might have even been fooled into believing him yourself, except for the eeriness in his tone, and the vicious grin upon his face.)

And so, in this fashion, the trial continued, bearing to the stand, before the council and those in attendance, one degenerate witness after another, all brought forward to testify; and with each new lie Faron's grip around his scepter tightened. And as well, he seemed more enlivened with each new deceit. Even once, he blatantly laughed aloud during a portion of testimony wherein no reasonable person would have.

Yet, to give it the air of legitimacy, this show of a trial took several more hours. During which time, the girls were being shuttled back and forth through the over-brimmed city streets. They were brought before seemingly every mid-ranking officer who was not presently in attendance at the trial, none wanting to give a direct order, and each passing that responsibility onto someone new who'd had, "...more jurisdiction over the matter..." or, "...would know better how to handle this sort of thing." Till at last, the head gatekeeper, who had begun their wanderings already tired and was by now sweating profusely in the noonday sun, decided to give his own ruling on what should be done, and turned about to bring the girls to the Court of Decrees, and to the trial: which had been going on for some time by then.

Yet meanwhile in the hall, the court officiant was in full voice, readying the council and the king for his closing address. His final speech to the council was pompous, self-serving, and not at all fun to listen to by most standards. And as so, for those reasons, I've decided not to put it down into writing. Except to say this: that he spent rather a great deal more time in pleasantries, thanking those high ranking officials who'd either, "taken time from their most honorable and worthy duties" or who had, "traveled at great length" to be there that morning, and he spent considerably less time discussing the seriousness of Corwan's case.

Until, at long last, he concluded his statements with these final words, "You have seen, gentlemen, today, by the honorable testimony of these present witnesses..." [Here some braver men who were left on the council, and some of those in the audience scoffed aloud or interrupted the speaker with their own interpretations of the day's events: and the validity, or lack thereof, of those present witnesses in question. But here again, the officiant chose to pay them little attention, only barely halting his speech in the slightest.]

"The evidence is weighed before us," he continued, his hands grasping the heavy gold chain that hung around his neck. "...and all those *truly* loyal to the crown can make only one summation."

He then, very soon after, called for a tallying of the members' votes. Which is, by tradition in Gleomu, a very involved and very tiresome process, wherein each member is called by name to stand and give his vote. And today's counting was no exception. It was as slow and as painful a process as it had ever been. With each new vote, Corwan stood amazed and in horror to see many in whom he'd trusted, or had thought to have trusted, rise and cast their votes against him: even counted among them some of his father's oldest and dearest friends.

It is a most disheartening thing (and true in all worlds as much as in our own), that the well adorned lies of those, the cleverest of soothsayers, can hold within their enchantments the ability to convince even the most goodly intended persons. And similarly, such was the case in court that morning: Those who had wished to be deceived from the start, for reasons of their own gains or purposed safety, were led into it with a renewed sense of blindness. And likewise, even sadly quite a few moral men (those of whom who'd never adequately developed within themselves clear means by which to measure truthfulness), were swept in alongside the rest; who knew truth, but for whatever reasons had chosen not to apply it.

And then, just as it is apt to do when things are at their darkest, and situations at their direst and most impassible states, something happened.

"Aren't you forgetting something?" an old, defiant voice blurted out from the midst of the crowd. It caught Faron and the officiant completely off guard. But Corwan had been expecting this voice and so he knew it from its first hearing.

The officiant tried to collect himself, as he turned quickly to scan across the crowded hall for the voice's origin, but could see no one. So then he, not meaning to be distracted by such a minor inconvenience, realigned the embroidered sash that hung around his shoulders, and turned again to oversee the tallying of votes. Only first dismissively commenting to the unknown voice as he did, "No... I assure you, sir. We have not." He said this like a false laugh, which inspired others in the council to laugh as well.

But this was broken abruptly when the man's voice spoke out a second time. It came from an older man, dressed in a green hooded robe, like a shepherd. He held a weathered staff in his right hand.

"I disagree," he said. "Isn't it in our traditions to offer members of the council a chance to speak, before the votes are counted?"

"Yes, yes..." the officiant answered, nervously fidgeting, pressing at the folds in his robe.

However, he spoke as one explaining an overly simplified matter to a child. And loudly, so that all the room could hear, he continued, "...but today's proceedings are a special occurrence, needing to be handled with sensitivity. For you see, it would not befit the dignity of this court [motioning behind him and towards Faron], nor that of our *dear* prince, to allow such... *interruptions*." At the end he gritted his teeth for the word 'interruptions', and gave a hard look at the man, clearly implying that he had not the patience for any further disturbances. And he turned back again to watch over the voting, which still continued.

But the hooded man would not be stopped. "Well then, if that's the case..." he spoke out again.

Corwan could see a clear shiver go across the officiant's back.

"Sir, like I said-" his voice grew stern.

"Do not attempt to lecture me, Malliff!" the man in the shepherd's robe roared, throwing back his hood, revealing his long silvered hair. "You do not know the first thing of dignity, and yet you intend to be my teacher."

The crowd was utterly shocked by this sudden outburst, and all turned instantly to see the man's face. Even the court officers, and all those of the council were in breathless awe, for they all knew him at once.

Faron, however, was much slower to respond. Being that he, in his mind, had already begun celebrating the victories of the day, and for a while now had not shown concern for much else. But in the instant he saw the man's face his greedy stupor lifted.

"Seize that traitor!" he exclaimed.

For as you may already have guessed, the common man in the crowd who was now standing in direct opposition to Malliff (the court officiant), and to King Faron himself, was none other than General Gamel, who'd snuck himself into the assembly that morning at Corwan's request.

Then at the king's direction, the guards pushed their way through the thronging crowds, encircling Gamel with drawn swords.

"I am not the traitor, Faron," he said with authority, while still scanning the eyes of the guards who circled around to see if any meant to strike at him. "How easily you seem to forget the laws, when they do not fall in your favor. It is unlawful to arrest a member of council before his trying."

"Then I will make my own laws!" cried Faron.

"Then you are no king," Gamel announced, and spit towards the throne as a sign of contempt.

For this, Gamel may have likely been run through with the sword, except that just then the doors of the chamber flung apart with a thunderous reverberation.

"Stop. Stop everything..." the portly gatekeeper muttered, still deeply out of breath from their long walk that morning. He panted noticeably as he spoke, "We got new evidence."

CHAPTER TWENTY-FIVE

GUILTY

A nd so it was that Del and Mattie, Gamel and the Prince, were all made to stand before King Faron and the council on the afternoon of Corwan's trial. Indeed, the spectacle of it was a bit over-whelming. And Del thought again, that perhaps her plan was not as good as she first imagined it to be.

"I'm sorry," she whispered to Mattie, as they stood before the glaring king, waiting for the court officiant to at last settle the chaotic excitement of the people, and that of the council.

"Yes, well... the decent thing to do would be to at least tell me what you were up to," Mattie snapped back.

"I knew you wouldn't come along if I did... and I'd wanted you here with me," Del replied, speaking the last part of her words more softly.

Mattie's face was cross, and her eyes scowled. Del knew that she had wounded her deeply, in only the way that a true friend can do it.

"But you didn't even give me a chance," Mattie said.

The officiant's voice began to raise above the clamoring of the crowd. His voice whined as he ordered there to be quiet. Though this did little to actually restore any bit of ordered silence. What did seem to work, however, was a threat from Faron that the next man who spoke would be hanged.

And that, of course, brought peace almost instantly. For there were none so foolish as to distrust the king's rage.

"You've come back to spy us out, have you?" Faron said when the room was still.

Del's voice was dry, and she was nervous to speak in front of so many people.

"No, Your Majesty. We haven't," she replied.

Then the gatekeeper, who was still standing at an arm's length behind them all, broke in. "They've turned themselves in, Sire," he said, still huffing from their long walk.

"Well I can see that..." Faron moaned, annoyed by the man's unrequested interruption.

"No, Sire, I mean for the murder. They say they've killed King Reuel," he spoke again.

"What!"

Faron slammed his hands down on the throne. And his face turned instantly from a grinning arrogance to boiling fury. "That's impossible," he issued. Then, turning to Del, he said, "Child, how dare you make a mockery of my court with these lies."

Del spoke, but only out of habit, replying that she was not a child. Then one of the council members rose to question why they should not hear her confession.

And there Del stood, with all eyes fastened upon her, about to plead guilty to a crime that she had not committed, to save a prince she'd hardly known.

She spoke, and her words felt grainy in her mouth. "I did it. *I* killed him," she said, meaning to take full responsibility, and stepping forward to separate herself from Mattie.

The council stared at her, disbelievingly.

"It's true... We killed him, both of us," said Mattie, stepping forward, as well. "And we feel positively dreadful about it," she added.

But Mattie, however, was not a very competent liar (which, by the way, is an admirable trait). And so by all accounts, she rather hurt Del's cause than helped it. Yet she felt compelled to help as best she could. For she now understood the seriousness of Del's plans here, and would not have her to go through it alone. No matter what that meant, or to where that decision might carry them.

CHAPTER TWENTY-SIX

AFTER THE TRIAL

T hat evening, around sunset, the girls and General Gamel were led, hands bound before them to the center of the city. Seemingly every resident of Ismere, and all those visiting for the trial, were pressed together so tightly that it left little room, even for standing.

Both girls had been given a fair trial, in spite of all Faron's bickering about its outcome, and even with many in the council trying desperately to dissuade them from their confessions. Yet, in the end, there was little that could be done. And as much as it pained them to do it, the council gave a guilty verdict. But Gamel, on the other hand, was given a maliciously unfair trial. Brought about, I'd suspect, at least in part by all those in council who'd wished him harm, secretly in their hearts for these many long years, and had now finally been given the chance to see it out.

Back in the main square, there were jeers from some in the crowd as the three scuffled their feet across the stone pavings. Most in the crowd, though, had somber expressions, and the old women cried pitifully once they saw how young Del and Mattie were.

"Doesn't seem right," Mattie heard one of them say.

And they climbed the cold hard steps of a low podium in the center of the square. And the executioner's face was shrouded by a long black hood. A man from the midst of the mob yelled something indecipherable, and many in the crowd began to laugh at their expense. Looking out over the people Del felt guilty, not for the murder of King Reuel, of course not for that, but now for the murder of her friend.

Up on a high platform, to the left of the podium near an ornately designed statuetted fountain, Faron perched in all his regal splendor with Corwan to his left, surrounded on all sides by armed guards bearing the crest of the golden eagle, the symbol of the royal family.

From the looks of it, they had done very little that day to squelch the king's rage; Corwan was still a prisoner, whether by title or not.

"*This is not fair,*" Del thought. It was by no means the glorious martyrdom she'd envisioned. And perhaps, like all martyrs, Del now knew full well the pains of under appreciation.

"Do you hear that?" Mattie whispered suddenly.

"We've nearly an hour left on our time," Del replied. "You're imagining things."

"I am not. And anyways, it's not that sort either. It's a lower sound, like an ocean almost..."

Oddly, now that Mattie had pointed it out, the noise became apparent, and Del could not fathom how she'd not noticed it before. But the reason for this was because it had been increasing in volume. At first, the faintest hum above the crowd, but now it was more like a distant train, Del thought. One that from the sound of it you knew was very large and must be headed in your direction.

The guards led the girls to the front of the podium, and placed heavy blindfolds over their eyes. The last face Del saw before the world went dim was Corwan's, and he had given her a sad, pitiful look. (She would not have enjoyed such a thing on most occasion, but here she felt as if she'd rather deserved it. And at least, if she were going to die for someone in a world that was not her own, she found it was nice to know that she'd be remembered.)

Then, the blindfold covered her eyes, and the world was dark. She could feel herself being made to kneel on the coarse stone. She regretted not setting the time for sooner, and thought about how they could've been gone by now if she'd known better.

"Del?..." Mattie's voice sounded scared as well.

"I'm here," Del replied.

And she thought of all the people she might never now see again: Mattie, her mother (and that roaring noise she'd heard before grew louder).

And she thought about her father, and if she would ever see him again. And she felt bad for hoping that she should, as if she were, in a way, breaking her mother's trust, who told her, "...not to believe in such fairy tales," but she couldn't help hoping for it. At this point, it seemed to become the most natural thing she could believe in. That perhaps, if this fairy tale land had existed, and it was as real to her as her own, then maybe heaven would exist, in some place yet undiscovered; and perhaps, it may be realer to her, when she had gotten there, than any world she had yet known.

But there was no death, at this time, and the roaring noise she had heard earlier began to take on a peculiarly human characteristic. Del lifted up her hands and pulled back the blindfold. The roaring flooded into the square. A sea of armed men poured through every street like a stream, filling the center of the city beyond capacity.

The scene was that of complete chaos. Across the way Del saw a fuzzy little creature, dressed in child's armor, clamor onto the back of an empty horse cart. He cupped his hand to his mouth and yelled something, but she could not make out what he'd said over the clashing of swords, and the tempestuous confusion that had enveloped the entirety of the city.

CHAPTER TWENTY-SEVEN

A NEW FIGHT

"Charge!" Meris yelled, as loud as his little voice enabled him. He had been much out of the practice of battle for some fifty years, and, in a somewhat unrelated way, had gained a healthy amount of weight since his younger days, but today he felt like a new pup.

(For you see, good reader, this had been the plan all along. This was the message Corwan had sent back to Gamel on the night before his trial, "...to gather an army for the attack." And also, that they should make it seem to Faron that he had already won, and therefore cause him to lower his guard. This they had done, and what a magnificent attack it was.)

Since well before dawn, Meris and Radcliffe, Gamel's right hand man, were out in the streets of Ismere, sneaking from house to house, entreating those known to still be loyal in their hearts to Corwan, and to the late King Reuel. But of all the men they found, their final count numbered less than two hundred. Henceforth, it was for this reason they came rushing into the square yelling as gloriously as they had, to bring about confusion, and to make themselves seem to be a much larger army than they actually were, but it had worked.

Within seconds of the attack, there was such chaos in the square that no one, including Faron, could tell with any accuracy how many men fought; nor, more importantly, which side was winning, and this made things remarkably easy for them. As it happened, many of the king's chiefest guards surrendered even without a fight, and of those who remained, because they had been caught so completely by surprise, only a few lasted much after the first blows.

So that oddly, in the end, it was Meris who did the most good. Holding on tightly to his wobbly helmet with one hand, he ran valiantly through the stampeding masses, slashing at calves and ankles, and jabbing the thighs of any who dared oppose him, only narrowly missing some of his own men in the process. From the tops of the crowd it was truly a sight to see. To the left and right, all around the plaza, guards would fall bellowing in pain, without warning and with no attacker in sight.

So then, from the onset, it seemed as though the only one with a real fight on his hands was Corwan. Once Faron saw his haughty plans quickly unraveling before his eyes, he drew his sword, as most tyrants will, meaning to strike his brother dead then and there, but missed, only barely slicing Corwan's right shoulder as the young prince leapt away from his brother's wrathful blade.

And so, after several brief moments of unrest, when for the most part the citizens and much of Faron's army had been subdued, Corwan was still in full battle, trying desperately to deflect his brother's bullish swipes. In good fortune, he'd managed to retrieve a long sword that had been abandoned by one of Meris's recent victims. Still, the weight of the blade was too much for him, especially with a wounded shoulder, and that made his right arm too weak to be of any good. And what is worse, he had no armor and Faron had, at least, some pieces of show armor across his chest and legs.

There was a brilliant clashing, as Faron attempted by brute strength to knock the sword from his brother's hands, but in the king's reckless fervor he left an opening for Corwan to slash at his side.

Yet, his success did not last long. With a few more thrusts and swipes the prince was knocked to the ground, a deep gash upon his leg, and his sword flung from his grasp. It landed with a splash in the fountain behind him.

Corwan's eyes widened. His breath was labored, and his face was deeply saddened. Faron smiled viciously, as though he had won, and reared back to deal his final blow, but stopped short. Dropping his sword, he cried out in agony.

"You devil rat!" he cursed, grabbing Meris by the scruff of his neck, and with his other hand pulling a miniature sword from his foot. Meris kicked and squirmed. He bit violently into the king's thick leather gloves, but with little effectiveness.

"Afraid to fight me like a man, are ya?" Meris said, exhausted from the struggle.

Faron laughed and grinned with excitement. "Ha! The little beast speaks," he said amusingly to those around.

"Yes. And I'll do more than that if you set me down," Meris shot back in response.

"And let you run away?"

Faron pointed the tiny sword at Meris's belly. "I'm no fool, little mouse."

And he went to run him through, but was thwarted yet again. Only this time, by a large graveled stone flung squarely at his brow. A line of blood streamed down the king's face, and he stammered, falling with a heavy thud onto his back and the hard cobbled stones.

At the sight of this there was a glorious cheering. When they saw Faron knocked from his feet, all those who'd remained in the square, Gamel's army, and even some of the King's hired guards, gave a joyous hurray. (For, it would seem, that all Mattie Hardy's long hours of practice at cricket, a game which held no warm place in her heart, had finally paid off; And she was an excellent throw, although she hid it quite well.)

Del kicked the bulbous tyrant in his side, but he lay as still as a grave. "Good shot, Hardy," she said, though Mattie just smiled at her work, peering over the fallen king. Meanwhile, Gamel went straight to mending the prince's wounds. He tore a strip of cloth from his tunic, and synched it up high on the young man's leg.

"*Ahhh!*"

Del felt a tug at her ankle, and Faron's eyes opened with an evil gleam. Mattie and Meris rushed to pull her free, but there was an awful ringing sound, followed by blinding light. All four were shot like a bolt into the sky, and they were gone.

CHAPTER TWENTY-EIGHT

A DEADLY PERIL

"Here. Quickly! Turn this," a small, frantic, earthy voice said to Mattie.

The window room was blackened dark. And the girls fumbled through the pitch starless room, pitifully endeavoring to do all Meris's orders. Though their eyes were still helplessly blinded by the glare of light traveling, so that Meris had to do most of it himself. (For he was far more used to this sort of thing, having lived under ground, in lightless tunnels, for the majority of his lifetime.)

Faron groaned. They could hear him moving.

"What day is it here?!" Meris yelled, flipping through the giant almanac.

"The thirteenth," Del quickly replied.

"No, it's not anymore. It's the fourteenth," Mattie answered. She was still at work, as Meris ordered, feverishly winding up the globe crank. Inside it ticked and whirled. From deep within, you could hear its mechanisms begin to awaken.

"Hurry, Meris..." Del implored. She'd noticed the king had grown very quiet now, and that worried her.

"I can't read the numbers," Del exclaimed, bending low over the globe, straining to make out anything in the darkness of the room.

The little ground dweller sighed aloud, hurriedly jumping from the desk, then up onto the console, turning and repositioning the dials as fast as ever. In his frustration he asked rhetorically, 'Why any humans had eyes at all, if they'd never seem to use them?'

Then, with the last dial and switch, the room began to glow. From out of the painting, the heavenly bodies of stars shone their light. And although night rested in its darkest hours here in our world, within the window room the light began to brighten.

Meris froze, suddenly. His nose twitched, and he stood up straight on his hind legs.

"Look out!" Mattie cried.

The sharp ringing of a knife went hissing by Del's ear, and stuck deeply into the globe's wooden trim. Bravely, Meris sprung from the console, his claws outstretched. But with a swipe of his gloved hand, the king batted him from the air, flinging him lifelessly across the room.

Without a thought, Del put her hands to the globe. Light beamed into the room, between her fingers. And she ran at Faron, striking at his wounded side with all her might. He seized her wrists, and the two rose up into the air, an orb of light forming around them. The evil king was vastly weakened by his injuries and disoriented, yet, even still, he remained many times her size. He drew his thick, dark gloves around her neck. And then, they vanished, into the outer reaches of space.

Stars flew by them at a dizzying pace. She kicked at his gouged foot. This lessened his grip, but only enough so that she could breathe. She could not break free.

Her eyes grew dimmed, and the stars began to hide their rays. They came to rest on an icy plane, on a ridge overlooking the snow entrenched canyons of a frozen wasteland, on a distant unfamiliar planet, and that was the last Del saw, of Faron, and of that world.

And seemingly pleased with his murderous work, the evil king let go of the girl, and went to find some place of refuge within that world of unforgiving ice. Though this was not the end for her, to be left cold and alone, and unresponsive, on an icy snow drift; For there was a light that had been growing within her for sometime, and if Faron had only turned around he would have seen it.

A minute later, there was a force that rattled life back into her lungs. Opening her eyes, the enormity of the universe sped by her in an instant. And she landed on her back, again in the window room, sputtering and gasping for air, her dear friends by her side.

In the morning, not much after sunrise, Mattie was called down to the Governor's office. Her meddling roommate, Margaret Thudman, had finally snitched her out; And although Del had not also been called, the two went boldly, hand in hand to receive of their fate, and they never told a word to anyone about where they had been.

EPILOGUE

That next fall, after two quarters of nearly constant punishments. That had only at last managed to amend themselves when finally Mattie's parents offered, as a sign of peace one might say, a considerably sizable donation to the Mayfield charitable funds. And after many more grand adventures with Meris and Corwan: in the window room, in Gleomu, and in the worlds beyond, the which that could not be fit within the pages of this book. It was during this time that Del received a letter.

One very unseasonably icy morning, in early fall, when the air lay dead and still, Del was given a letter. This letter came not by the normal means, however, but had been hand delivered to her by her professor. It bore the seal of her mother's sister, and the contents of which was not at all pleasant.

It read as follows:

My Dear Delany,

Your mother is very ill, and the doctors inform me that her sickness is that of a new fever that they have not the ability, nor the medicine to cure. Also, they do not expect her to last on through the winter. I am, indeed, sorry for your recent losses, and, I assure you, your mother and I have been dear to each other in our own way as well.

Albeit presently, you should make your affairs in order, gathering your luggage, and within three days a cart will come from Crawley to take you on to a hospital in Sutton. There you will remain until your mother's passing, and after which you will come to live with me in Bedford. My deepest condolences.

   Sincerely,

   Aunt Merrill

Del would not eat that day, nor the day after, and spoke only pieces of it to Mattie. Only enough to say that she had to leave soon, and did not know when, or if, she would be back.

On the eve before she was to leave, Del took a candle and a sack of her things, and crept across the lawn to Greyford. She opened the door only slightly, so to not make a sound, and snuck up the stairs and through the halls to the attic. And for a long time she did nothing, but blankly stared at the painting in the window room and the rich cities of Gleomu. And then, wiping a final tear from her eye she resolved in her heart to do it, turning the dials sharply, setting her time for as long as she could be away, three hundred and sixty-five days, a full year to the day and hour.

"Where are you going, child?" a thin earthen tone spoke, somewhat like a whisper.

"I'm not a child, squirrel..." she retorted, wiping her face to make it seem as though she had not been weeping.

Meris stepped closer, his chubby cheeks now fully grayed with age, and his voice more graveled and tired. "Under normal circumstance I would agree, but now you are acting like a child, and so that's what I'll call you."

Her eyes furrowed. "You wouldn't understand..." she spoke, fighting back her tears. "My mum is ill, horridly so, she'll die too, just like my father. I can't go back."

"I can't..." she repeated, and slumped to the floor clutching her knees to her chest.

He stepped yet again closer, and placed his tiny paw on her shoulder. "You can't run from this, Del."

"No? And why can't I?" she said crying.

"Because your mother needs you, most of all now," he said. "It is selfish of you to think differently."

After this not much else was said between them, and Meris remained with her until morning.

This is very near the end of our story dear reader, only a few things more deserve mentioning: First, it is an unending amazement how well Del's mother's sickness had improved her mood. For although she had grown weaker physically, in most areas, she was yet stronger in others, and this other strength more than made up for her present weakness. So that, in the end, some two or three months longer than had been anticipated, she died, a much happier woman. And that secondly, when Del was finally brought to live with her aunt and cousins in Bedford, it became instantly apparent to her that her relations cared only for inheritances, and for little else.

And that following spring, when she was back at Mayfield, a year removed from her mother's death, Meris died as well, being old and too full of life, one hundred years old to the day, as years were counted in his world (which by comparison, in our terms, accounted for roughly eighty-seven years, as we would count them).

And on that same afternoon, they buried him, in the shade of a young beech tree that grew near the house. This was not the sort of occasion either girl could find the words for, and so they said nothing, but patted his small patch of earth firmly, for he had been to them a true friend.

And this last part, it would seem, has become more like a legend now than exact truth, and so I will tell it as such:

In her final year there at Mayfield, on the first night, of the first week, of the first quarter, Delany Calbefur vanished from her room, never to be seen nor heard from again.

Since then, it has largely been decided (by the authorities, and those adults who seem to think they know much better about these sorts of things), that Delany had long since suffered disillusionment at the loss of her parents, and had, within herself, developed a sense of dissatisfaction: with her school experiences and with her present home life. And had therefore, through no fault of anyone's, decided to run away.

Among those adults who'd kept an interest in her case, this seemed to be the popular reason for her disappearance, and was spread around amongst the local papers, in varying degrees, during the weeks that followed. Yet, for the girls at Mayfield however, theirs is a different view of what happened that night, a more sinister explanation if they can tell it right.

They say that she'd been murdered (but as to how exactly, or for what reasons, no one has ever agreed); And these disputes, about the facts, have lent themselves to many magical and mysterious variations of as to what truly happened that night, each girl swearing to the validity of her own creation, and some more believably than others.

Though this one haunting detail has been amongst the tales since the very beginning and as such, is most often taken as truth: They say that every year, near the first night, of the first week, of the first quarter, precisely one year from the day on which she first disappeared, just after midnight, you can see a small gable window in the old Greyford house light up like the day, but only for a brief second, and only if you watch for it without blinking.

And very often, girls who know more honest versions of the story will end theirs like this: That the only one who knew what really happened to Delany that fateful night, was her best friend, Mattie Hardy, and *that* she's never told to anyone, not a living soul.

THE END OF BOOK ONE

The Story Continues... in **A Prince of Earth**

★★★★⯨ 4.5 stars on Goodreads

If Timothy Hayfield had known the mysterious secrets
his grandmother had kept quiet all these years,
and if he'd known the peril that would await him
during a seemingly average summer's holiday in Mayfield,
then he might have stayed behind.

But who can tell what simple decisions
may lead to grand adventures?
In the undiscovered corners of his family's estate,
he would find the fates of kings, and of worlds,
that are hung in the balance.

In places that would take him beyond our world,
there would be battles, and valor, but only if Timothy wished it.
For you see, this was a choice, not a requirement:
A simple decision that would make him a Prince of Earth.